D0009932

Contents

1
A noise in the night

Suddenly, unaccountably, David was wide awake.

For a moment he lay still in the darkness, every sense alert. Something had awakened him, but what?

It must have been a noise, he reasoned — a loud one to have roused him so thoroughly. But there was no sound now. The night was quiet.

He moved his head to look at the soft green glow of the clock radio. Two fifty-three. He turned the other way, to the faint square of the window, but it was almost as dark outside as it was in the room, the light of the full moon blocked by heavy clouds. David could see nothing from where he lay.

He pushed back the single cover and crossed to the window and peered out. An owl hooted from the black mass of trees that stretched away from the back of the store, its plaintive call carrying clearly on the still air. Apart from that — silence. Still, David was not satisfied. He had heard *something*, he was sure of it. He had to check outside.

He felt his way to the door and took his

dressing gown from its hook while he found his slippers with groping feet. Then, taking a flashlight from the night table, he opened the door and descended the stairs to the store. Below him, the dim night light distorted the shadows of canoes in racks, casting eery patterns on the floor. In the deeper shadows of the shelves that lined the walls he could make out the tents, camp stoves, sleeping bags and other items that canoeists heading into Algonquin Park came to rent or buy.

The store window faced the opposite way to the one in his room. Through it David could see the yard light filtering through intervening trees and reflecting off the cars parked in the lot. There was no sound, no movement.

David released the lock on the front door and stepped outside into the warm September air. The owl hooted again. Somewhere a skunk had been disturbed and had reacted. Otherwise the night was very still.

David circled the store, checking the windows, flashing his light into the gloom of the encircling trees, passing it over the canoes beached upside down on the river bank. Nothing had been touched. He turned to the cars awaiting the return of their owners, but there was nothing to suggest that they had been disturbed either.

He stood for a moment, irresolute, uncertain what to do, toying with the idea of checking with the night clerk at the lodge. Then he decided against it. Whatever had disturbed him had gone now. The night was as serene and as peaceful as always.

He was about to reenter the store when he heard the sound of a vehicle approaching. Headlights gleamed through the trees, causing towering shadows to weave and bob in a grotesque dance as a pickup truck with a canoe on the roof of the cap pulled into the brightly lit parking lot.

David watched from the shadows with interest. It was not unusual for trippers to arrive during the night hours. Generally, though, they waited in their cars for daylight — but not this time. Two men set about unloading the canoe and carrying it to the low dock. Then they brought out backpacks and fishing gear from the cap and loaded them into the canoe.

David wasn't near enough to distinguish the words as the men spoke to each other in hushed tones, but it certainly looked as if they intended to start out in the darkness. Well, good luck to them, he thought. The shallow river with its tortuous channel and lurking rocks was tricky enough in broad daylight.

One man stepped carefully into the canoe, manoeuvred his way to the bow and took up a paddle. This time David heard the other man's words.

"Never mind the paddle. I can manage. We'll have the current with us anyway. You've got to shine that light so I can see where we're going."

You can say that again, thought David. He watched as the man pushed off, propelling it into the stream. They were moving down river, the light probing the darkness, when one of the men made an odd remark that carried clearly.

3

"So the little bear is leading us to the loon."

Now what was that all about? wondered David. A reference, perhaps, to the lodge — Little Bear Lodge, where he was working for the summer. But "loon"?

If there was a reply to the remark he didn't hear it. Mildly curious, he watched the bobbing light until it disappeared around a bend in the river. Then, yawning widely, he let himself back into the store and climbed the stairs to his bedroom. He realized as he dozed off that he still didn't know what had awakened him.

*　　*　　*

In the gloom of the trees a man waited motionless for a full ten minutes after David had returned to bed. Then he shoved a gun into his pocket, put his hands under the shoulders of an inert figure at his feet and dragged it deeper into the silent blackness of the forest.

*　　*　　*

His first customer was already waiting when David let himself out of the store the next morning.

A man in a plaid shirt, fishing hat and jeans was sitting on the river bank, puffing on a cigarette. When he heard the door he flicked the butt into the river and stood up.

"Good morning, young fellow." He was a big man with deep-set, heavy lidded eyes that gave him a sleepy appearance. "Are you open for business?"

"No, not really. We don't open till eight o'clock. But if you'd like to make an early start I don't mind making an exception."

"No no, I'm in no hurry. It's just that when I saw you come out of the store I thought it must be open."

"Oh, I see. No, I live upstairs. If you're really in no hurry I'll carry on up to the lodge for breakfast."

"Fine. In fact I think I'll join you." He fell in step beside David. "This job of yours," he said, pleasantly. "It's a summer job isn't it? But school started last Monday . . ."

"The store stays open full time for a week after Labour Day, so I got permission to stay around. I finish today at four o'clock. After this week it's only open on weekends until Thanksgiving, when it closes down for the winter. One of the staff at the lodge will take over when I'm gone."

"So you're finished today? Does that mean you'll be going home tonight then?"

"No," said David, wondering vaguely why this man was so interested in his movements. "I have special permission from my principal to have the next two weeks off because a friend is coming to visit me from Scotland. She won't be arriving till Monday, though, so I'm staying here for the weekend. Well, not here, exactly. I'm going to take a canoe trip down the river."

"*She*? Aha!" The man's lazy eyes twinkled. After a moment he asked casually, "So I suppose you must know this area well, then?"

"Pretty well, yes. This is my second summer

5

on the job. And one other time I went with the scouts on a canoeing trip that started at Kiosk and ended here. So, yes, I guess I'm pretty familiar with the area."

"Ah." They reached the lodge and went in to the dining room where they sat at a table by the window, the man choosing a chair that looked out on the parking lot.

"By the way," he said, "my name's Fred Johnston."

"I'm David McCrimmond. Where are you from, Mr. Johnston?"

"Call me Fred. I'm from Toronto. How about you?"

"My home is in Woodstock —"

"Morning, David." The waitress stood by the table, smiling. "The usual?"

"Yes, thanks."

Fred ordered sausages and eggs. When the waitress had gone he turned back to David and said offhandedly, "If you're familiar with the area, maybe you've heard of a place around here called Loon Lake?"

David frowned. Loon Lake. That sounded awfully familiar. What had that man on the river said last night? *The little bear will lead us to the loon.*

"No," David said, "I've never heard of such a lake."

Fred had noticed his hesitation. "You're sure?"

"Quite sure. The river out there, the Matta-makos, leads into Lake Mong. If you want, you can travel throughout the park from here — hundreds of kilometres of lakes, rivers and portages. I have a map of the whole park down at the store. We can take a look at it, but I'm sure there's no Loon Lake."

Conversation ceased with the arrival of breakfast, but after a few minutes Fred broke the silence.

"I was wondering," he said, "if you would be interested in making a little extra cash."

"Extra cash! Sure. I can always use more money. What is it you want me to do."

"It isn't much." Fred withdrew his wallet, extracted a business card and handed it to David. It bore the legend *Regal Continental Insurance*, and the name *Fred Johnston*.

"Uh, oh." David looked up warily. "You're not selling insurance, are you?"

Fred chuckled. "No, don't worry. I'm not a salesman. I'm an investigator."

"Oh?" David's curiosity was aroused. "What do you investigate?"

"Suspicious claims. Say there's an unusual fire: was it accidental — or the result of arson? A person dies under strange circumstances: was the death due to natural causes — or something else? That sort of thing."

"I see. Sounds exciting. But what is it you want me to do?"

Fred was about to reply when something outside caught his eye. He was suddenly tense. David turned, curious. A man had just emerged from a car that had pulled into the parking lot. He was probably in his forties — short, with a bald head and neatly trimmed brown beard.

"David," said Fred, his voice low, "you can begin to earn that money right now. See that man who just arrived?"

"Yes."

"Okay. Find out his name and what his plans are."

"What? How in the world am I supposed to do that?"

"Oh, you'll think of something." Fred took four dollars from his pocket. "Give that to the waitress. I've got to go. I'll meet you down at the store in half an hour and explain. It's a case I'm working on for my company." He turned and walked quickly from the room by the rear exit.

David looked after him, confused and a little excited: an investigator working on a case, wanting his, David's, help. But how do you go about learning a stranger's name and his plans?

Okay, he thought, why not the direct approach. When the man was seated, waiting for his breakfast, David could welcome him.

"Good morning. We're pleased to have you come to Little Bear Lodge. My name is David McCrimmond." Expectant pause. He would be obliged to answer, wouldn't he?

"Good morning, David. I'm John Smith."

"Pleased to meet you Mr. Smith. I'm in charge of the store down by the river. We rent everything you'll need to take a trip into Algonquin Park. Would you be interested?"

"Sorry. I'd like to take you up on that but I'm just on my way through to Ottawa. Maybe another time."

8

There. Just like that. Name and destination. It should be easy.

As it turned out, it was even easier than that. From his seat David saw the newcomer pause at the front desk. After a short conversation the clerk handed him a key and pointed down the hallway towards the guest rooms.

So, thought David, he's staying at least one night. After he left the dining room he stopped by the desk.

"Morning, David." Mike Marino, the night clerk, was checking his files before going off duty. "This is your last day, isn't it?"

"That's right. I'm through at four o'clock. Then I'm heading down river for one last weekend in God's country before going home. By the way, was there any kind of disturbance last night — or rather this morning about three o'clock? A noise of some sort?"

Mike thought back, then shook his head. "A truck came in about that time. A pickup truck. It didn't stop here. Went right on down to the landing. They had their own canoe, so they might not need your services. You must've seen them this morning."

"No, I saw them last night. Something woke me before that and I was out looking around when the truck arrived. They took off down river right away."

"In the dark?"

"Yes. Wonder how they made out. Anyway, it was just a few minutes before that that something woke me. There didn't seem to be anything wrong, though."

Mike shook his head "I don't know what it could have been. It's pretty quiet now the summer's over. We only have four rooms in use — five now, with the man who just checked in."

"Oh, yes, I saw him. Is he staying long?"

"Undecided. Two nights anyway. He's an artist. Might be canoeing into the park. He seemed interested."

"Ha. I'll have to do a selling job on him. What's his name?"

Mike checked his files. "Webb. Austin Webb."

"Right. I'll watch for him."

2

The Newbury necklace

"Austin Webb, eh? So that's what he calls himself now."

David looked at Fred curiously. "What do you mean, 'now'?"

"It's an alias. The police know him as the Ferret. He's a jewel thief."

David's pulse quickened. "But what —"

"Sit down. I'll explain." David perched expectantly on the counter top. Fred pulled up a chair and sat facing the open door. "About six years ago there was a series of jewellery thefts in the Rosedale district of Toronto. The thief was an expert who took only the best pieces in each case and left the cheaper stuff behind. One piece, a diamond and emerald necklace, was stolen from the home of Isaac Newbury, the racehorse magnate. It was insured by our company for three quarters of a million dollars."

David whistled. "Three quarters of a million!"

Fred nodded. "To make a long story short, the thief was caught before he could dispose of the jewellery and sentenced to ten years in prison. Trouble is, not all the loot was recovered.

The Newbury necklace was never found and we had to pay up."

"Three quarters of a million!" repeated David in awe. "But if the rest of the jewellery was found, maybe he didn't steal that particular piece at all. What did he say about it?"

"Oh, he denied stealing it all right. Admitted to taking the rest of the stuff — he hadn't much choice faced with the evidence — but denied going near the Newbury place."

"What do you think? *Did* he take the necklace?"

"Sure he did. I investigated it myself with full cooperation from the police. I have no doubt in the world that he stole the Newbury necklace."

"Then what happened to it?"

Fred grinned. "He's a sharp man, is our Ferret. He knew the police were onto him and it would be only a matter of time before he was caught. Figured the law would be satisfied if they found the bulk of the loot, so he hid the most valuable piece where he could retrieve it later — after he'd paid his dues, so to speak. A prison term with time off for good behaviour, and he'd still be a young man on his release. With the proceeds from the sale of the Newbury necklace he could live comfortably for the rest of his life."

"But the necklace would still be 'stolen goods' wouldn't it, and pretty difficult to dispose of?"

"No trouble for him. No doubt he has underworld connections. Fences. Or he might break it up and sell the stones separately. He wouldn't get full value if he did that, of course, but he'd still be a rich man."

"And that man up at the lodge who calls himself Austin Webb is really the Ferret. But you said he was sentenced to ten years in prison, and yet you also said all this happened only six years ago."

"Don't forget time off for good behaviour. He was a very good boy."

"But what is he — what are you — doing here?"

"Treasure hunting. The necklace is somewhere in this area. I want to beat the Ferret to it."

David digested this information slowly. "How do you know the treasure is around here? And how are you going to beat the Ferret to it? Why don't you just let the Ferret retrieve it and then have the police arrest him for possession of stolen goods or something?"

"To answer your last question first, I may have to let it happen that way, but not if I can help it. Justice moves very slowly, you know, and the necklace would be tied up in the courts as evidence for ages. And as long as the necklace is tied up, so is our money — which means the loss of additional thousands of dollars in interest. Besides the police have long since given up on the case. Once the Ferret was convicted and put away, the law was satisfied.

"As to the rest" — Fred drew a crumpled piece of paper from his pocket and smoothed it as he spoke — "just before his arrest, the Ferret went on a trip up north. The police were shadowing him, but he shook them off in North Bay.

They picked him up two days later in Mattawa. I believe he hid the necklace in the interval.

"Since his release from prison two weeks ago, I've been keeping an eye on him. This is the first time he's come up this way. When he took a motel room in North Bay, so did I. I even chatted with him — he doesn't know me from Adam — and he told me he was coming here for a holiday. When he was out I, er, visited his room and found a map. This is a copy." He handed the paper to David.

A roughly drawn oval was labelled *Loon Lake*. From it, a vertical arrow pointed downward to a spot marked with an X.

From the X, a horizontal arrow pointed to the right and ended at a vertical wavy line. The point at which the arrow met the wavy line was marked with another X. That was all.

"That's a map? You're sure you didn't miss anything?"

"No, that's it. Rather sketchy, isn't it?"

"Sketchy! I'll say. Not only that, but there's no Loon Lake anywhere around here, anyway. Come to think of it, six years ago there wasn't even a Little Bear Lodge here for that matter."

"That doesn't matter. The river was still here, leading into the park. It *is* disappointing that the maps don't show a Loon Lake, but then, as far as I can make out, there's no Loon Lake listed anywhere else in Ontario, either, so it doesn't really matter."

"It doesn't? How do you figure that?"

"Obviously he made the name up for himself, so it could be any lake. This map wasn't drawn for me or anyone else. The Ferret drew it six years ago just to make sure he would remember where he hid the necklace."

David nodded slowly, looking at the map with renewed interest. "That makes sense. And since he's come here, it probably *is* in this area. But I don't see how you're going to beat him to it if this is all you have to go on."

"Well, maybe it's not as hopeless as it seems. I have to deduce what I can from the map — and hope he gives me time. This is the way I figure it. Why did the Ferret choose Algonquin Park as a hiding place? Because it's a protected area. With cities spreading and new communities springing up and roads being pushed through everywhere, he had to find some place he could be sure would be undisturbed in ten years. One answer — Algonquin Park. So he shook off his pursuers in North Bay and came here.

"He probably 'borrowed' a canoe from one of the nearby summer cottages and paddled down into the park. My guess is that with time running out and one place as safe as another, why go too far? I think the lake he calls 'Loon Lake' must be the first one he came to. So what lake would that be" — he turned to the map of the park — "Lake Mong.

"For some reason, perhaps to confuse anyone else who might happen to see the map, he calls Lake Mong 'Loon Lake.' Okay so far? Now, this arrow pointing downward, or presumably south, means he went in that direction. We have no idea how far. Maybe a few metres, maybe several kilometres. Anyway, he came sooner or later to something he identifies with an X. Question is, what is it that he identifies with the X?"

"That wouldn't be *my* first question," David said. "Instead I'd want to know what point he started out from. Lake Mong is pretty big, you know. I'd guess at least eight kilometres long. The arrow is drawn a little to left of centre, but I doubt if that means anything. Probably only the Ferret knows for sure."

Fred shook his head with a touch of impatience. "I don't know where he started from," he admitted. "That's something I'll try to figure out when I get there. Right now I'd like your ideas as to what this X might represent. Something he would still recognize years later, obviously. An extra tall tree maybe? The remains of a trapper's cabin? What?"

David shrugged. "If he knew anything about the forest at all he would know that it's changing all the time. Natural evolution. Trees die and fall or burn. Other trees grow. Beavers build dams and create lakes. There's really only one thing you can count on remaining the same — rock."

"Rock?"

"Yes. Perhaps a ridge of bedrock. Or more likely one big rock that has been there since the ice age, left behind by receding glaciers."

"Ah." Fred appeared impressed. "Very good. Well, whatever it is, I hope I recognize it. When I do, I turn east and keep going till I come to a river or creek. I would guess that squiggly line represents a creek. That's where the necklace is hidden."

David nodded slowly. "You make it sound

easy. I wish you luck. But why are you telling *me* all this?"

"Because I want your help. The Ferret, or Austin Webb, will have to come to you to rent a canoe. At least I presume he will. He certainly didn't bring one with him. I want you to try to delay him as long as you can. Think of some reason why he shouldn't go into the park for a few days. The longer the better. I'll need all the time I can get. I doubt if he'll be in any hurry after all these years. Also" — he stood up, walked to the door, looked around outside, and came back —"also, no one must know I've been here. *No* one.

"When you come down the river later today, look for me. I'll be camped somewhere on the south side of Lake Mong — probably about the halfway mark. When we meet, you can tell me how successful you were in delaying the Ferret, and whether any other suspicious looking characters arrived at the lodge or set off down river."

"I don't understand." David was perplexed.

"It's a well-known fact in the underworld that the Newbury necklace has never been found. I'm sure I'm not the only one keeping a close eye on the Ferret now that he's a free man again."

The underworld! David shivered. And three quarters of a million dollars at stake! What have I got myself into *this* time?

*   *   *

Not much, really, decided David resolutely a few hours later as Fred Johnston rounded the bend in the river and disappeared from view. Nothing compared to last year.

17

Inevitably, Fred's map had reminded David of the map he had found last year in a dead man's boot; a map that had led him into some hair-raising adventures in the Scottish Hebrides; a map that had also led him to Sandy McLeod.

He pictured her now as he had first seen her, dressed as a deck hand on a trawler with wind tossed, red-brown hair and cheeks flushed by the cold. Then he pictured her as he had seen her in the great dining hall, dressed like a lady, with the light from flickering candles reflected in her dancing eyes.

Sandy, who would be arriving at his home in Woodstock on Monday. No, he wasn't going to get involved in anything, no matter how exciting, that might in any way interfere with his being home in time to meet Sandy. He would keep his eyes and ears open and report to Fred, of course, but that would be the extent of it.

* * *

His first customer after Fred had left was the Ferret himself!

David looked at the little man with interest. He walked with a quick, lithe grace, light on his feet. David could imagine him climbing ivy covered walls, tiptoeing softly across thick carpeting in the very room in which his victims slept.

"Good morning," said David courteously. "Can I help?"

"Perhaps," returned the other cautiously. "I'm thinking of taking a trip down the river into the park to do some painting."

"Ah, well, I can rent you a canoe and everything else you'll need, except food. You have to get that at the lodge. I hope you have some warm clothing. It can get pretty cool at this time of year."

The Ferret waved the issue aside with a touch of impatience. "I have plenty of warm clothing. Anyway, I expect to be gone only one night. Two at the most. I'll just be doing some preliminary sketching this time." His eyes constantly moved as he spoke, over the cars in the lot, along the road to the lodge, even to the line of trees across the yard.

"I'm expecting a friend to join me. We'll be going together. He should be here by now."

A friend? That might be of interest to Fred, thought David. Aloud, he said, "May I make a suggestion? Things are pretty busy right now. There'll probably be a lot of people going into the park for the weekend, and quite a few who are in there now will be coming out today or tomorrow." This was a bit of an exaggeration, since the real rush was already over, but under the circumstances it seemed like an appropriate thing to say.

"I imagine you would prefer peace and quiet in which to do your sketching. You're more likely to get that if you wait till Monday or Tuesday. If you and your friend have the time, that is."

"That sounds like a good idea," the Ferret said with a wry smile, "but can you guarantee us good weather?"

David laughed. "I can't make any promises, but there is a good chance it'll hold."

"Actually, I can't make any arrangements at

all till my friend arrives anyway, so we probably will wait till Monday or Tuesday. Well, thanks for the advice. I guess I'll come back later."

The Ferret turned and walked away towards the lodge. David felt pleased with himself. I've given Fred the whole weekend, maybe longer, to search for the necklace without having to worry about the Ferret, he thought. And without having to worry about anyone else for that matter, he realized a moment later. If there *were* others, they would also have to wait till Monday or Tuesday in order to follow the Ferret into the park.

* * *

The rest of the morning was quiet. A group of six scouters came in to the store to register their trip — a two week safari into the interior — but since they were self-equipped they had no need of David's services. A family of four dropped in to reserve a canoe for a river trip the next day. Three groups came out of the park and returned the equipment they had rented. David left the canoes by the river in the hope of renting them again later.

Early in the afternoon, David was busy mending an air mattress in the store when a car identical to his father's pulled into the parking lot. David noticed it, but since it was a common model and colour, he paid no further attention to it. A few minutes later a familiar voice spoke from the doorway.

"Well! I was hoping for a warmer welcome than this."

David dropped the tube of rubber cement, whirled around and stared.

"Sandy! How in the world . . ." He stood up, looked at her for a moment, then sprang forward and caught her up in a hug that lifted her feet off the floor. "Sandy! Am I ever glad to see you!"

3

Sandy

"Well," Sandy said again, breathlessly, "that's more like it." He released her reluctantly and she kissed him lightly as he lowered her to the floor. He stepped back to look at her: the same auburn hair with the fire deep in the curls, the sprinkling of freckles across her small nose and the laughing blue eyes that had enchanted him in Scotland. A long moment later he became aware of his father watching from the doorway with a grin and a twinkle.

"Dad! But I thought . . . Sandy, we weren't expecting you till Monday."

"I know," she said, still breathless, "but I was on stand-by. Somebody cancelled and they called me yesterday, so I telephoned your family to see if it was okay to take the earlier flight, and they said it was."

"We knew you wouldn't mind," said Mr. McCrimmond. "It seemed like a great opportunity to show Sandy a part of Ontario she wouldn't see if she arrived later, especially since it's your favourite country. Today's your last day on the job, isn't it?"

"Yes," nodded David, still dazed by this

happy turn of events. "I'll be finished at four o'clock. I was going to canoe into the park till Sunday, but that doesn't matter now. This is much better."

"Wait a minute. You can still do that. In fact we've planned on it. We've brought an extra sleeping bag and tent for Sandy. She can go with you."

"Hey! That's great! Sandy, you'll *love* it."

Mr. McCrimmond came over to the counter and picked up a map of Algonquin Park. "Don't plan too strenuous a trip, Davie. Sandy denies it, but she must be pretty tired after her long flight. On top of that, we had to leave home bright and early this morning, and it's a tiring ride." He opened the map out on the counter top. "I would suggest," he said, "that you don't go any further than Loon Lake."

"Oh yes, I wouldn't —" David stopped abruptly. He stared at his father. "*What* did you say?"

"I said you shouldn't go any further than Loon Lake."

"That's what I thought you said." David stared down at the map. "Dad, where in the world do you see Loon Lake on that map?"

"Right there." He pointed.

David shook his head. "But that says in plain English, Lake Mong."

"Ah, that's where you're wrong. In plain *Ojibway* it says Lake Mong. Which in plain English is Lake Loon."

"You mean — well, I'll be. I never thought of that. Dad, how do you know that?"

"Don't forget I taught school on an Indian reserve for three years. That river out there, the Mattamakos, that's Ojibway too. Do you know what Mattamakos means?"

"No, what?"

"I'll bet the owner of Little Bear Lodge knows. Mattamakos means the Trail of the Little Bear."

The *trail of the little bear*. Again David remembered the two men who had started down the river in the middle of the night. What had the man said? "The little bear will lead us to the loon." That made sense now. Not that it indicated anything other than that the man apparently knew some Ojibway. But Fred Johnston might be interested in hearing about those two men.

His father was talking again. "We'll get the tent and sleeping bag out of the car and then I should be on my way. Anything else Sandy needs, you can rent from the store."

Less than an hour later the two friends were sitting alone on the jetty, catching up on each other's news.

"This is wonderful," said David, "just sitting and relaxing together and not worrying about submarines and caves and smugglers. Your Uncle Rory couldn't come with you, eh?"

"No." Sandy shook her red curls. "The authorities provided him with another ship and he's outfitting her and doing trials. But he sends his love and hopes we have a nice *quiet* time together."

"We will." David sounded determined.

"Nothing will disturb us this time. Not even a stolen necklace."

"A what?"

"Oh, nothing." He changed the subject quickly. "What are your first impressions of Canada, Sandy?"

She wrinkled her nose in thought. "Two things," she said. "Size, and trees." She wrapped her arms around her legs and rested her chin on her knees. "We're taught in school that Canada is a big country, but until you've seen it you've no idea. Your parents met me at the airport and showed me a little bit of Toronto before going on to Woodstock."

"What'd you think of Toronto?"

"Very impressive. Especially when you look at it from the CN Tower of course. But I liked the view in the other direction better."

"You mean the lake?" He nodded. "I knew you would."

"Yes. Cities are all very well, but I love the ocean best. You know that. And the lake, like everything else, is so huge it's like an inland sea. I liked the countryside around Woodstock too. Gentle and green, and the beautiful trees, and the farms with all the cows and — oh yes, I saw The Cow."

He grinned. "I *told* you Woodstock had a statue of a cow."

"I know, but I don't think I really believed it till I saw it. Then there was the trip up here this morning. My goodness, we could have gone all the way from Inverness to England, but when your dad showed me how far we'd gone on a map of Canada, I couldn't believe it. We'd hardly moved."

"I know. Rather overwhelming, isn't it? I haven't seen a great deal of the country myself yet. But this is my favourite part: Northern Ontario, with all its hills and lakes."

"And trees. I didn't know there were this many trees in God's green world."

"I wish you could stay a little longer. A few weeks from now and you would see this country in all its splendour. Gold and brown and crimson splashed all over the hills and valleys."

Sandy grinned. "You sound like Uncle Rory talking about the Hebrides. I think this weekend is going to be fun. You know I've rowed a boat before, but I've never paddled a canoe. I suppose it's quite different."

"Yes, but you'll soon get the hang of it. We go down this river for about eight kilometres — that's about five miles to you — then into the lake Dad mentioned. Loon Lake. We'll find a spot to camp there. Then we'll just wile away the weekend. Maybe swim a bit. And maybe fish a bit. I'm not a keen fisherman though. How about you?"

Sandy shook her head. "Not really. I'm not too fond of cleaning them. Maybe that's why."

"When we get to the lake, I have to look up a man who went down earlier this morning. His name's Fred Johnston. He's camping on the south shore." David hesitated, then he said, "I'd better tell you why."

Sandy listened to his account of the morning's happenings. When he had finished, she shook her head in wonderment.

"David, what is it about you that attracts excitement?"

"About *me*!" David shook his head in protest. "Not just me. About the *two* of us, maybe. Yes, I think it must be when the two of us get together. I led the tamest life imaginable until I went to Scotland. Then when I got within range of you, bingo! I was up to my neck in international smuggling. And what happens this time? I lead a perfectly respectable, quiet, boring life until you get within a certain distance of me, and bingo again! I find myself involved in a jewellery robbery. Rather mundane, I admit, after international espionage, but still not your everyday happening. No!" he corrected himself resolutely. "*Not* 'involved.' I'm going to keep *out* of this mess."

"I think you said that last year at one point."

"I guess I did. But I mean it this time. How am I ever going to get to know you if I only see you under pressure? No, I'll make my report to Fred Johnston as promised when we find him, and that's *it*." He made a final, chopping motion with his hand.

Sandy looked at David cornerwise and said "Hmmm," rather doubtfully. Then she said, "What do you have to report?"

"Just that the Ferret won't be going down to the lake before Monday at the earliest, so he'll have all weekend to search for the necklace undisturbed. And that no one suspicious — that is, no one who might be a crook on a treasure hunt — has put in an appearance."

"Don't speak too soon. Here's a car coming now."

A station wagon approached from the direction of the lodge. It turned into the parking lot and drew to a halt as close to the river as possible. Two people got out, stretching.

"Still no one suspicious," said David. "That's Mr. and Mrs. Penrith. Annual visitors." He scrambled to his feet and helped Sandy up. "A couple who believe in camping in comfort. Come and meet them."

The Penriths were almost a matching pair, except that she was blond and his crew cut was dark. Both were short and a little overweight, but both carried themselves well. And they both wore glasses. Hers were fashionable and his horn-rimmed with snap-on shades. They were, Sandy guessed, in their early fifties.

"Good afternoon, Mr. and Mrs. Penrith. Welcome back. Remember me from two years ago?"

"Of course. David, isn't it?" Mr. Penrith met him with outstretched hand. "We missed you last year."

"Yes, I was on holiday in Scotland. This is a good friend I met over there. She's here on a return visit. Sandy McLeod, Mr. and Mrs. Penrith."

"Clive and Dorothy," he corrected. "Pleased to meet you, Sandy. We come here every year to rent a canoe from David, or whoever takes his place when he runs off to Scotland. Your biggest canoe as usual, David."

"It's all ready for you." David pointed to where the canoes were lined up on the bank. "Have you brought anything new this year?"

"No *additions* to our gear, if that's what you

mean. I think we have all the camping gadgets available. But we couldn't resist a few replacements and improvements. We bought a new tent. Bigger. Family size. Though there's still only the two of us, of course."

"So that meant we had to get a larger heater," added Dorothy, "and a better radio. One with a tape player. What are they called, Clive? Some odd name."

"Ghetto blaster." Clive chuckled. "Not that we're going to blast any ghettos, or anything else. News reports and soft music, that's what we want it for."

"And you brought the tarpaulins, did you? And all the other accessories? Then I take it you won't be going any farther than Lake Mong again?"

"No. At our age we prefer to avoid portages." said Dorothy. "Besides, there's really no point in going any farther, at least not for us. There are enough birds and fish and plants and trees and rocks and animals at Mong to keep us going for years."

"My goodness," said Sandy, "you do have a lot of interests."

"Yes, I suppose we do. Birds are my speciality. Lapidary is Clive's."

"Lapidary?" Sandy wrinkled her nose in thought. "Isn't that something to do with jewellery — precious stones?"

"That's right," nodded Clive. "We have a jewellery store in Kitchener. But when we're here it isn't precious stones we're interested in, just pebbles."

"Yes," said David, enthusiastically, "you should see the bracelets and necklaces and things he makes out of beach pebbles. He cleans them and polishes them and brings out the most beautiful markings in stones that you and I would trample into the sand without a second thought."

Clive grinned, pleased with the compliment. "I have one or two with me, if you'd like to see them —"

Dorothy cut in, "Not now, Clive. They're at the bottom of one of the bags, and after all the trouble I went to when we were packing, I'm not going to disturb anything till we reach our campsite."

"That's okay," said David hurriedly, "Sandy and I are coming down to the lake later today. We'll drop by for a visit tomorrow and you can show them to her then."

"Very good," nodded Clive. "They're in there somewhere. I'm just not sure where. But if you're coming to the campsite, it doesn't matter."

"Yes, do come," said Dorothy. "We'll watch out for you and put the kettle on for coffee. Or would you prefer tea, Sandy?"

"Tea every time. How did you know?"

"Oh, you being from Scotland and all."

4

Suspicious characters

If there was nothing to worry about where the Penriths were concerned, the opposite was true about the next group to arrive.

They came in a beat-up van that lifted noticeably when the front passenger got out. He was a huge middle-aged man of enormous girth with a head as bald as a bowling ball and almost as round. The driver was younger, with curly blond hair and muscles straining against his thin cotton T-shirt. A third man in the back had enough hair for all three. Black and curly, it fell to his shoulders, grew low on his forehead and curled around the openings of his shirt. He was small and wiry and quick.

They stood by the van for a few minutes, looking around and talking. They seemed especially interested in the truck that had come the night before.

When they approached the store, David noticed that the big man moved lightly and effortlessly despite his bulk. His voice was surprisingly cultured.

"Good afternoon, young man. And Miss.

We're planning a fishing trip into Algonquin Park. What's the procedure?"

"Come inside and I'll explain."

The big man followed them in, leaving the other two to wait at the door.

"Normally," said David, "you report to the park ranger, but he won't be here for a week, so you report here instead. First you have to fill out this card. Now that the season's over, there's no quota, but there's still a fee of two dollars per person per night."

"Right. Let's see." David watched as the man filled out the card with the pen provided.

He put his name down as Max Rogo. When he came to the space for the vehicle licence number he called over his shoulder to the younger man who had been driving. "Erik, what's the licence number?"

"CX8 180."

Max Rogo wrote that down. "Trip start date? Trip end date? What if you don't know how long you're going to stay? What then, young man? We don't know *how* long we'll be staying. Depends on how the fish are biting. Does it matter?"

"I don't think so. I guess you'll be staying at least for the weekend, so why don't you put Sunday down for the trip end date. If you stay longer, you can make up the difference when you return."

"Fair enough. So that'll be twelve dollars for now. Right?" The big man counted out the money and put it in the envelope supplied. "I take it everyone going into the park has to fill out one of these?"

"That's the idea."

"Er, we're looking for some friends we're expecting to meet here. They may have gone on ahead. Any chance we could see the cards that have been filled out in the last day or two?"

"Sorry. They go into that locked box over there. I don't have a key. The ranger will open it when he comes back next week."

"I see, but perhaps you can help us anyway. That pickup truck over there, I think maybe it belongs to our friends. Do you know who came in it and when?"

"Two men. About three o'clock this morning. They had their own canoe, so they didn't need me at all. They launched it then and there and took off down river."

"At three in the morning?" Max Rogo raised his eyebrows. "Then they didn't fill out one of your cards, eh? Trying to sneak into the park without paying, d'you think?"

"Not necessarily. The river itself isn't in the park. It empties into a lake right at the park boundary. Here, I'll show you on the map. If they don't cross the boundary into the lake, there's no permit required."

"Hmmm. Could be our friends all right. Charlie always said he prefers river fishing to lake fishing. Well, as you can see we've got nothing but our fishing gear. You'll have to supply us with everything we'll need."

"Sure thing." David winked at Sandy. "This is my kind of customer. Let's see now. One canoe or two?"

"Just one. Erik's the only one with any experience, so we'll all have to go together. I hope you have one big enough." He turned and called to Erik again. "You and Tony better look after this. Get everything we'll need."

Erik nodded. He came in and spoke quietly to Rogo. "I'm sure that's Varga's truck. Why don't you see if you can raise him on your speaker?"

Rogo nodded. "I'll try. Depends how far away they are. I'll try out in the parking lot." As he spoke he unclipped a walky-talky from his belt and extended the aerial. He went out, leaving Erik and Tony to look after supply details.

"One canoe." David had picked up a list and was checking off the items required. "Paddles and life jackets. Tents. I would suggest two two-man tents. Three sleeping bags —"

"What about animals?" broke in Tony.

"Animals? You mean pets?" David looked up from his list, distracted. "Oh, you mean *wild* animals. Nothing to worry about. There are wolves and moose and bears of course —"

"*Wolves?* And *moose?* And *bears?*" Tony sounded nervous.

"You might hear wolves around dusk, but you'll never see any," David assured him. "And as long as you don't argue the right of way with a moose, you've nothing to worry about. If you meet a black bear, just use your common sense and go the other way. Quietly. Ten to one he'll do the same, only faster. Of course, bears are always on the lookout for a free meal, so you should keep food out of reach overnight or when you're away from camp. Do you know how to do that?"

"Put it in a tree," suggested Erik.

"No, not *in* a tree. Hang it over a tree *branch*, three metres off the ground and two metres away from the trunk. That'll keep it safe from both bears *and* racoons. Never keep it in your tent. A hungry bear will rip a tent to shreds in no time." David smiled at the worried look on Tony's face. "Don't worry," he said. "As I say, just use common sense. Actually, *skunks* are the biggest threat."

"*Skunks!*" Tony blanched. "I hate skunks. There aren't many of them around are there? I can't stand them. I'd rather take my chances with a bear. At least you can walk away from a bear without getting sprayed."

"You'll be okay," said David cheerfully. "Common sense again. Just treat skunks with respect. They don't go looking for trouble, so don't give them any and you'll be all right."

Enough said, thought David, this guy's scared silly. He dropped the subject and turned his attention back to the list of supplies.

In a few minutes he had checked off all the items the three would need for a weekend in the park.

"There's a five-and-a-half metre canoe on the river bank, that's the largest we have. I'll just go out back and check it for paddles and life jackets. Be back in a few minutes. Coming Sandy?"

They left the two at the counter and went out the back door.

"What do you think?" whispered David. "Would you classify them as suspicious charac-ters?"

"Definitely," said Sandy. "So they're probably quite innocent. All the same, I think you should tell your detective friend about them. I thought you'd already checked all the canoes."

"I said that as an excuse to come out and talk." David was looking around. "Where's the big guy? Do you see him?"

"No — yes. Over there in the parking lot." Max Rogo was standing in the middle of the parking lot with his back to Sandy and David, speaking into his walky-talky.

"Good. Now here's my idea. We slip quietly back into the store and get behind the partition — and listen. I especially want to hear what that guy Max Rogo says when he comes in."

"You're sneaky," accused Sandy, but with obvious approval. "Look, he's shutting down his aerial. He must be finished."

"Okay. Let's go."

They crept quietly back into the store through the rear door and to a spot where they were hidden behind a partition but within earshot of anyone at the counter.

They were just in time to hear Max Rogo speak as he came back in. "Where are the kids?"

"Gone out to check the canoe. Any luck reaching Varga?"

"Yes. They're here all right. Down by the river mouth where it empties into the lake. That way they can see anyone who goes by."

"Good. What about the Ferret?"

David and Sandy exchanged excited looks.

"He hasn't shown up yet, so we're ahead of him. He could be up at the lodge right now."

"So whadda we do? Wait and follow him?"

"No. Varga says the Ferret hasn't gone by yet, but someone else has."

"Who?" Something in Rogo's voice had alerted Erik.

"Dozey Johnston."

Johnston? David frowned. They must mean the insurance investigator. Of course. Those sleepy eyes! Dozey — an obvious nickname.

"Dozey Johnston! What the hell's he doing here!"

"I can tell you this," said Rogo, "it's no coincidence, that's for sure."

"But if he's gone ahead without waiting for the Ferret, he must know something we don't."

"That's right. So we won't wait. We'll go in now and find out what Dozey's up to. Meanwhile, Varga will stay where he is so he can let us know when the Ferret arrives. Are we just about ready to go?"

"Pretty near, but they don't have no food here. We have to get that from the lodge."

"Okay. Tony, you go and look after the food. I'd better not go near the lodge in case the Ferret's there. He doesn't know you. Where're those kids."

David gripped Sandy's hand. They tiptoed back to the rear door, then turned and entered the store noisily.

"Your canoe's ready," David announced. "Paddles and life jackets are aboard. It'll only take a few minutes to gather the rest of your gear."

Half an hour later, David and Sandy watched the heavily laden canoe set out. It sat deep in the water, mainly because of the bulk of Max Rogo amidships, and was propelled on an erratic course by Erik in the stern, with some clumsy help from Tony at the bow. The canoe moved sluggishly, Erik's inexperience at manoeuvring becoming more and more evident.

"They should have taken two canoes," said David a little uneasily. "But with only one semi-experienced canoeist I guess they couldn't. I hope they aren't in the middle of the lake when a wind comes up."

"They'll manage," Sandy said drily.

"You know that Dozey Johnston Rogo was talking about?" David said anxiously. "That has to be Fred. Remember what I said about his sleepy eyes? It has to be him."

"They knew all about the Ferret, too," Sandy added uneasily, "so they obviously know about the necklace."

"We really should warn Fred about them." David hesitated, then he added, "I wonder how come they know him so well?"

"Didn't you say he's an investigator? Maybe he's investigated those three before and they haven't forgotten him."

"That's possible," said David. "No doubt *someone* has investigated them before now."

"You don't suppose they would harm Fred, do you? If he found the necklace, I mean."

"No, no. They'll just look for a chance to steal it from him." But David's voice lacked conviction. "I don't like it," he confessed, after a moment. "The sooner we're able to warn Fred, the better."

5

The hunt is on

The tranquil river flowed sleepily between wooded banks of hardwood and evergreens. In places it was quite shallow, so that Sandy had to keep a sharp lookout from her position in the bow for rocks thrusting their heads above the surface. Many of them already showed coloured scars where less wary canoes had bumped and scraped against them.

Dragonflies swooped above the river while Sandy and David glided silently past water lilies and arrowheads. Bluejays scolded from the leafy boughs and woodpeckers sent their urgent messages echoing across the forest.

Sandy had little to do other than maintain a lookout. Seated on the front edge of the seat, her knees on the floorboards, she practised paddling the way David had shown her. David too had an easy time of it as the gentle current carried them along.

They had been travelling for maybe twenty minutes when David broke the silence.

"Just up ahead there, Sandy, we're going to make a detour. The main channel bears right, but we'll take that secondary channel to the left. It rejoins the main stream later on."

"Shouldn't we go straight to Fred's campsite?"

"No. I was thinking about that. As long as we talk to Fred today sometime, it doesn't really matter when. He certainly won't find the necklace this afternoon, and they won't do anything until he does have it. So we might as well take our time and enjoy ourselves. After all, this *is* supposed to be a holiday."

"That's fine by me," Sandy responded happily. "This is so beautiful. I'm just loving every moment of it."

The secondary channel was so narrow at first, there'd have been no room to pass if they'd met anyone coming the other way. But then the river started to widen and grow deeper, the water reaching out and spilling over the banks into the aspens and sedges. Suddenly Sandy saw why.

She looked back at David. "What is it? A dam? It looks like someone's made a dam."

"Not someone, beavers."

David edged the canoe ahead till the bow nudged the top of the dam. From her seat Sandy could see how it was built with sticks, rocks and mud, gently sloping on her side and steep on the other.

"It's marvellous! And you mean to say animals did this? But why? Why do they build dams?"

"To form ponds — which sometimes become actual lakes — so that they have places to build their lodges. This dam is quite recent, so there aren't any lodges here yet. Actually, it's hard to tell if they're still working on it or not. They may even have abandoned it. Anyway, when they do build the lodges, they build them with sticks much the same way the dams are built, only they're built in the middle of the pond. They're high enough to reach above the water, but the entrance is located near the bottom. That way, the beavers can eat and sleep above the waterline, safe and secure all year round."

"Fascinating." Sandy pointed to some tree stumps. "Is that where they've been cutting the trees down?"

"Yes, aspens mostly. Isn't it neat? Quite the little engineers! Well, I just wanted you to see this. We'd better move on."

"Don't we have to go back?"

"No, we go ahead. You'll get wet feet, but I hardly think that's going to bother the Sandy I know so well!"

"Of course not. But how? There's a metre drop here, and anyway, we don't want to destroy the dam by climbing all over it."

"Trust me. First, you'll have to move back a bit in the canoe to raise the bow."

It was awkward when Sandy tried to move. The canoe dipped precariously, first one way, then the other. But finally, as Sandy managed to make her way back towards the stern without mishap, the bow lifted and David paddled ahead until the canoe overhung the dam.

"Now," he said, "step out."

Sandy looked at the mass of twigs and mud doubtfully. "D'you think it'll hold me?"

David grinned. "Try it," was all he said.

Sandy tentatively put one foot down and then stood on top of the dam.

"Marvellous," she said again.

"Right," said David, "here's where you get your feet wet. Jump down to the shallow side, but be careful. The stones under the water will be slippery."

Sandy jumped carefully into ankle deep water. With her help David edged the canoe ahead until he too could step out onto the dam and follow her. Then they lowered the canoe.

"We'd better carry it for a bit, it's pretty shallow for a few metres, but it soon gets deep again."

*   *   *

Their detour brought them back to the main channel at a point where the river drifted along slowly and quietly. They let the current carry them for a few minutes, lying back in the canoe without paddling, admiring the scenery, until Sandy sat up with a cry of disappointment.

"Look at all those dead and dying trees," she said, pointing. "What a shame! What happened?"

David manoeuvred the canoe to the bank and grabbed some tree roots to counteract the current.

"It's not all that bad. It's caused by an insect called the spruce budworm. But the budworm also attract birds, lots of them. Listen." He let the canoe drift again with the lazy current and the sounds of dozens of birds came to them, calling, singing.

"Dying and decomposing trees attract other insects too, which in turn bring in more birds. And of course, new growth will come eventually, and then deer and moose will move in until the forest becomes too thick again. And so the cycle goes on. That's one of the great things about Algonquin Park. Nature is pretty well left to work things out her own way, and she does a good job of it."

David began to paddle and they moved on a

little faster. It wasn't long before they spied a column of blue smoke and caught a tantalizing whiff of frying fish.

"Camp ahead," reported Sandy.

"Yes." David instinctively lowered his voice. "These must be Max Rogo's friends, the ones camping near the river mouth."

"Are we nearly there then?"

"Just about."

Soon they saw a tent back among the trees, and a canoe beached upside down on the river bank. Two men were coaxing a fire under a frying pan and kettle.

David waved. "Hi! Smells great. Good fishing?"

"Not bad." A bearded man held up a string of silvery fish. "Brook trout."

"I'd call that pretty good," shouted David as they glided past. To Sandy he said, "For me that would be excellent. Well, there's the lake ahead. Lake Mong, or Loon Lake, according to my father. We're now in Algonquin Park."

The lake lay like a silvery jewel in a great wooded clasp. One lone island raised its rocky spine above the surface of the water. The hills all around, low to the north but rising higher in the south, were clothed in varied shades of green, with here and there a thread of gold and a patch of crimson giving promise of the brilliant fall colours soon to adorn the forest.

"You know," said Sandy as they nosed out into the expanse of water, "when your father said we were coming to a park I pictured carefully cut lawns and flower gardens, with swings for the children and maybe a football field."

"Disappointed?"

She turned and looked at him reproachfully.

"Hardly. This is far more beautiful. I'm totally smitten."

"I knew you'd fall in love with it. It *is* beautiful, isn't it?"

David stopped paddling and allowed the canoe to drift while they both drank in the scenery around them. Then, reluctantly, he spoke again. "First things first. We'd better paddle along the south shore and find Fred's camp. See that peninsula jutting out ahead? He'll be somewhere in that vicinity. After we've found him, we'll pick out a site on the north shore. The farther we are from him the better!"

As they followed the south shore they met two canoes heading out and greeted the occupants with cheerful banter. They waved to a lone fisherman and passed a campsite where children were splashing in the water. Otherwise there was little activity. When they neared the peninsula, they spotted a campsite with two pup tents and a beached yellow canoe.

"I'll bet that's our three friends," said David. "Let's go and see how they're getting along."

"Won't they be suspicious?"

"Oh, I don't think so. As you've already seen, trippers tend to be very friendly and ready to help. I'm just being neighbourly."

They moved in closer and saw Max Rogo approaching along the shore, his walky-talky still on his belt and a pair of binoculars around his neck. Tony was attending to the camp stove. There was no sign of Erik.

"Hi," called David, moving close in. "How are things going?"

"Hello, young fellow. Is this part of your service, checking up on your customers?"

David laughed. "No. Actually you're not even

my customers any more. There'll be someone else there when you go out. We're on holiday now ourselves. I just thought I'd check that everything was all right. It isn't always easy the first time out."

"Oh. Very good of you. No. No problem. We're fine."

The words were civil enough, but his manner suggested that any lingering would be unwelcome. David nodded. "That's good. Have a good weekend."

They pushed off again and soon rounded the point. There on the other side of the peninsula was Fred's campsite. David recognized it by the canoe, a red four-metre fibreglass model beached beside a tent.

"That's Fred's camp all right, but I don't see any sign of him. Let's check it out."

They moved the canoe in close until David could step out into ankle deep water. The tent was closed, a camp stove and a tin of fuel were beside it, and a knapsack was slung in approved fashion from a branch. He walked around the tent, looking into the nearby trees, but there was no sign of Fred.

"He's not here," David reported. "We'll go set up camp ourselves and come back later."

David headed the canoe diagonally across the lake. "I know where there's a good site for us. It's got a nice sandy beach — if it's not already occupied."

The site was deserted. They pulled the canoe up on the shore, climbed a low overhanging embankment and found themselves in a small open space with large trees all round.

David pointed to a faint pathway leading away from the site. "We're not entirely in the wilderness," he said. "Follow that path and you'll come to a privy. You know what a privy is? Probably an outdoor cluggie to you. Not exactly the Ritz, but it's better than nothing."

"Oh good," Sandy said. "In fact I think I'll check it out right now."

When she returned, David had his tent up. "What say we have supper first," he suggested, "then have another look for Fred. The camp stove's over there. It's easy to operate."

Sandy inspected the stove. "Looks simple enough. What do we do for water?"

He pointed to the lake. "No shortage of that. Better add a purification tablet, just to be safe. What would you prefer to do: set up the other tent or make supper?"

"Help me with the tent, then we can both make supper. Let me put the kettle on first, though."

"Great idea." Between them they had the second tent up in short order. Soon they were enjoying a supper of sausages, beans, instant potato, tea for Sandy and bouillon for David, eaten lazily, their progress watched now and then by a pair of envious chipmunks.

By the time they had finished and washed up, the shadows had lengthened noticeably. David took out a supply of nuts and chocolate for snacks later and then stowed the rest of the food in a knapsack, threw a weighted rope over a branch and pulled the container up out of harm's way.

"Okay," he said, "Let's check out Fred's camp again. I'll take my fishing gear in case we have to put in some time waiting for him."

There was still no sign of Fred, so they paddled leisurely out over the still, smooth lake to the island.

While Sandy watched, chin cupped in hand, David tied the canoe to a fallen tree that reached out over the water. Then he put a fat worm on his hook and dropped it over the side. Almost immediately there was a jerk on his line and he pulled in a small bass, dancing and glistening as it dangled from his rod. He freed it and dropped it back into the water.

Within fifteen minutes David had returned ten undersized rock bass to their more cautious elders.

"I think I'll quit while I'm ahead," he said as he laid the rod down in the bottom of the canoe. "If I'm not careful I might catch something we'd have to clean."

But he didn't release the canoe from its mooring right away. Instead, they sat in companionable silence as stillness settled over their world. The sun had disappeared behind the forest, its waning light silhouetting the spiky evergreens, deepening the blue of the sky in the east and washing the west with a red glow. One by one, stars appeared, winking and sparkling.

Over all there was a great silence and stillness. Suddenly the quiet was broken by the high, quavering call of a loon.

Sandy turned questioning eyes on David. "What was that?"

David grinned. "The call of the north. The voice of Algonquin. To be more precise, a loon." He pointed to where a pair of water birds floated, barely distinguishable in the gathering gloom. "I think I like that one sound more than any other."

He loosened the rope that held the canoe to

47

the root and dipped his paddle in the water. "We'd better have one more look for Fred."

They passed Rogo's camp well out from the shore, its location marked only by the occasional glow of a flashlight. On the other side of the peninsula they moved closer in to shore again. Fred's camp was still in darkness.

"Doesn't look as if he's back yet," said Sandy. "Unless he's gone to bed already. Do you suppose he has?"

"It's possible — no, wait a minute. The canoe's not there. He must've come back and gone out again while we were fishing."

"Then we've missed him. Do you think we should wait here for him?"

"Not if we can leave him a message. Do you have a pen with you, by any chance? And something I could write on?"

Sandy rummaged through her pockets. "I've got a pen, but nothing to write on. Just tissues. They wouldn't do, would they? "

"Just a minute." David took out his wallet and flipped through the contents. "Of course. Fred's card. Just the thing. Let's see." He thought a moment, then, by the glow of his flashlight he wrote on the card in a tiny hand:

Watch out for Max Rogo and gang camped behind you on the other side of the peninsula. He's after the necklace. He knows about the Ferret — and you.

"That should warn him. I'll leave this somewhere in his tent where he can't miss it."

It took David just a few minutes to paddle to shore and leave the message. "I stuck it on the front of one of his boots and left the boot in the middle of his pillow," he reported to Sandy with a grin. "I don't think he'll miss it. Let's go." They launched the canoe and headed back across the lake towards their own camp.

They were approaching shore in a leisurely fashion when Sandy turned to David, puzzled.

"It looks as if we've got company, Davie. There's someone at our camp. Look!"

6

Moon maid

Sandy and David could see the silhouette of one lone figure dimly in the darkness.

"Hey! Whoever it is has lit a fire. Who on earth could it be," David said, wonderingly. Flames crackled and danced in the circle of rocks at their campsite.

They soon had their answer. As the bow touched sand a man dropped down the embankment and came to meet them.

"It's Fred Johnston. We didn't have to leave a message for him after all."

"Welcome home." The man waded into the shallow water and helped them pull the canoe up onto the beach. "I have coffee all ready for you."

"Now that's a nice way to be greeted," grinned David, a hint of relief in his voice. "How did you find us?"

"I saw you from further along the shoreline when you called at my campsite earlier. I waved but you didn't see me. So I watched where you went and here I am. Who's this young lady?"

"Sandy McLeod. I think I told you I was expecting a friend to come from Scotland. She caught an earlier flight than expected and my dad brought her up here so we could have the weekend together. This is Fred Johnston, Sandy."

"Hello." Sandy shook his hand. "David told me about you."

"Good." They climbed the bank. Fred had a pot of coffee on a rock close to the flames. The logs on which David and Sandy had sat to eat their supper were drawn up nearby.

"I brought my own coffee and mug," said Fred, lifting the pot. "Hope you can supply the fixings."

A few minutes later they were sipping the steaming drinks when David said, casually, "Do you know a man named Max Rogo?"

Fred looked at him sharply. "Max Rogo? Oh, yes, I know Max Rogo. Big guy — bald as an egg. Why? What do you know about him?"

"I know he's here, camped right behind you, on the other side of the peninsula with two friends. They know all about the necklace and the Ferret. And they know you too." He hesitated, looking at the other questioningly.

Fred frowned. "Yes, they know me. At least Max does. I testified against him in court once, so I guess there's no love lost between us. Do they know I'm here?"

"Yes. Two more of his gang were camped by the river mouth and they saw you go into the park."

"At the river mouth? I did notice a camp there, but I didn't see anyone around. They must've seen me, though. And they recognized me too, eh? Damn! I'm getting to be too well known by the criminal element. I should've thought of that. Any other news?"

David told him all that had transpired since Fred had left that morning. Fred listened quietly. The news that the Ferret had been delayed obviously pleased him, and the presence of the Rogo gang didn't seem to bother him.

"Good," he said when David had brought him up to date. "You've been a big help. As long as I know what's going on, I think I can handle it all right."

"How about you," asked David. "Did you have any luck with that map? Or is it none of my business?"

"Let's say I'm encouraged. I'm almost sure I've found the first X on the map. As you suggested, a rock. A huge one all by itself on a hillside in the forest."

"How did you find it?"

"Tried to put myself in the Ferret's shoes. I reasoned he must've picked some obvious starting point from which to set out. The peninsula itself is the most logical feature to pick, so I tried walking due south of it, but I found nothing in that direction. Then I thought, maybe he used the island as a landmark, and went south of that, but with no success. Later it occurred to me that if he really wanted to go south it would be easier to go by water, so I looked for the deepest bay on the south shore. By deep I mean southward, not downward. And I hit the jackpot."

"You must be tired."

"Beat," he admitted. "It's been a long day and I've covered a lot of ground — and water! And I want an early start in the morning, so I'd better be getting back."

"What about the Rogo gang?"

"I'm not going to worry about them. Forewarned is forearmed. They'll be counting on me to lead them to the necklace. I'll make sure I'm up and off before they even know it. Well," he said, draining his cup and standing up, "thanks again for your help. Don't say anything about this to anyone for another week. That's all I ask. Have a good holiday. Enjoy your stay in Canada, Sandy."

* * *

"Well, he's a cool customer," said David after Fred had launched his canoe into the darkness. "I wouldn't be so nonchalant if I had the likes of Max Rogo on *my* tail."

"He doesn't want us to tell anyone," mused Sandy. "Personally I'd feel better if we could tell the police."

"What would we tell them? No one has broken any laws — yet. I guess he knows what he's doing. I'll bet he gives everyone the slip and finds that necklace tomorrow. Well, it's no longer any concern of ours, thank goodness."

* * *

Moments after Sandy and David left the note in Fred's tent and headed back across the lake, a man emerged from the nearby trees, slipped quietly across the site, opened the tent flap and crept inside. The soft glow of a flashlight showed briefly through the nylon, and then the man was out of the tent, the card in his hand. He closed the flap, looked around quickly and merged once more with the shadows. A few minutes later he handed the card to Max Rogo.

"What's this?" Max turned the card so that the flickering light of the fire shone on it. "Fred Johnston, Regal Continental Insurance. What is this! Who does he think he's kidding?"

"Yeah. Wait'll you see the other side." Tony was feeling pleased with himself.

Max flipped the card over. "I can't make it

out in this light. Pass me the flashlight." His eyes narrowed. "You got this out of Dozey's tent? Who put it there?"

"Those two kids who rented us our equipment."

"Those two teenagers?" echoed Max in amazement. "He's using *them* to spy on us?"

Erik spoke quietly from the shadows. "So what? They're nothing to worry about. *We* got the card, not Dozey. He still doesn't know we're onto him."

"That doesn't mean he ain't going to find out," growled Tony. "He's not at his campsite. For all we know, he might be talking to those two little punks right now."

"It doesn't matter," snapped Rogo. "Dozey's going to find out about us sooner or later, so we might as well assume he knows already. That's not the problem. Whatever happens, Dozey won't go running to the police, we can be sure of that. Neither will the Ferret. But the moment those two kids find out what's really going on here, you can be sure that that's just exactly what they *will* do. That makes them a threat."

"No problem!" Erik said with grim finality. He patted his hunting knife and looked at Rogo. "When?" he asked softly.

* * *

For the second time in as many nights, David woke in the small hours of the morning. This time, though, he wasn't jarred into wakefulness. Instead, he stirred, rolled over and pulled the sleeping bag about his ears. Then he rolled over again, onto his back, fighting a losing battle in his bid to stay asleep. Finally he opened his eyes.

He was vaguely surprised to see how bright the night was. The full moon, he thought hazily. He closed his eyes — then opened them wide, suddenly alert. A movement near his head, beyond the thin nylon of the tent. Some vague movement. Then the unmistakable snapping of a twig.

He was wide awake now, up on his elbow, listening, trying to hear above the thumping of his heart. A bear, he told himself. But it wasn't a bear. Bears didn't care who heard them. *This* was stealthy, breathless.

He pushed back the sleeping bag and edged on hands and knees towards the door, away from the sound. He would have to stick his head outside and try to look back the length of the tent to find out what was going on.

The full moon was riding high and bright, its lustre spreading out across the night sky so that only near the dark horizon were the stars visible. And it had laid a carpet across the lake that shimmered and rippled with the gentle movement of the waters.

"Beautiful, isn't it?"

David almost jumped out of his skin.

"Sandy!" he said, weakly. "Holy *smoke*, you startled me."

"Sorry. I was trying to be quiet so I wouldn't disturb you. I wouldn't make a very good Red Indian, would I?"

David laughed in relief. "What in the world are you doing, walking about at this time of night?"

"I think 'obeying the call of nature' is the delicate way to put it. It's so bright I didn't even have to use my torch. Isn't that a glorious moon? I'm really glad I woke up. I wouldn't want to miss this." She sat down on the ground at her tent door. "Aren't you pleased I woke you?"

David had to admit he was. He stretched out on his stomach, with just his head out the tent door, and propped his chin on his hand.

"It is beautiful," he agreed. "It reminds me of a poem I learned once, called *Moon Road*."

"Called what?"

"*Moon Road*. That." He indicated the path of moonlight across the lake. "Let's see if I can remember some of it:

What lies at the end of the moon road there?
The maid of the moon in her radiant lair,
With the stars agleam in her lustrous hair
and the teardrops in her eye."

Sandy wrapped her arms about her knees and gazed out on the scene. "Let's go and find her," she said.

"What?"

"Your maid of the moon. Let's go to the end of the moon road there and see if we can find her. Maybe we could wipe the tear from the poor girl's eye."

"Gee," David demurred, "that might not be such a good idea." He continued with the poem:

"Go, and I'll never again be free
Though each silvery ripple is calling me
Where the moon road shimmers across the sea,
And never again return."

"Never return?" asked Sandy. "Why not?"

"Because she's luring people to a fate worse than death — like Ulysses and the Sirens:

See her in silvery vapours dressed,
Calling me home to her own warm nest,
Calling, 'Come back to me and rest,'
Back to the moon-drenched skies."

"Moon-drenched skies," Sandy repeated, gazing up into the heavens. "I like that. What the heck! Let's go anyway. I'll do my best to preserve you from her clutches."

"You mean it? You really want to go out there? Now? Okay. Let's do it. Just give me a minute to get dressed. You'd better put on a jacket. It'll be cool."

Sandy was standing by the canoe, looking down the length of the moon road when David joined her.

"Almost looks as if you could walk on it, doesn't it?" she said.

"Try it," invited David as he manoeuvred the canoe into the water.

Sandy did, with predictable results.

"Just call me Peter. Sadly lacking in faith." She climbed into the canoe, sat on the thwart amidships and removed her wet shoes. "You'll have to do all the work, Davie. I'm going to preserve my energy in case I have to rescue you from the moon maid's clutches."

"No problem," agreed David with a smile.

They set off down the silvery path. Each dip of the paddle spilled drops of water that winked and blinked in the moonlight. Somewhere far behind them an owl hooted mournfully. From the far shoreline came the enchanting cries of two loons calling to each other. Sandy trailed her hand in the water and began to sing softly.

"What's that you're singing?" asked David when she paused.

"*An Eriskay Love Lilt*. In Gaelic."

"It sounds sad."

"Most Gaelic songs are."

They moved on dreamily till at last the shore loomed in front of them and the black trees reached long fingers into the sky, clutching at the moon. The shadows spread across the water, blotting out the silvery path. The canoe crossed the last winking ripple and nudged into the darkness.

"We're here," said Sandy. "The end of the moon road and no sign of the moon maid."

Her face was in shadows when she turned, but the moon lit up her hair like a halo.

"Let's go on and see if she's in the trees."

They ran the canoe up on the shore and stepped out. They were staring into the dense blackness ahead of them when suddenly a cry ripped the silence of the night, a tearing, inhuman cry deep in the forest.

7
Murder!

Sandy clutched David's arm. "What was that?" she asked in a frightened whisper.

"Oh, nothing to worry about." David replied. He tried to sound nonchalant, but his voice was shaky nonetheless. "Some creature just caught its prey."

Sandy shivered. "Let's go back."

The magic had suddenly gone from the night. David turned to launch the canoe when he stopped short, staring out across the lake.

"Sandy, did you see that?"

"What? What did you see?"

"A light back at our camp. Just a flash, like a flashlight."

"No — No, I didn't see anything. Are you sure? What could it be?"

"It could be Fred back again to make coffee for us," he said lightly. "Or it could've been my imagination."

They started back slowly and silently, their carefree mood destroyed. David kept his eyes on the spot where their tents were pitched, but there were no more flashes, no signs of life. The moon still shone, bathing the scene in a ghostly glow.

They had just climbed the embankment to the campsite, when David stopped short.

"Someone *has* been here."

Sandy clutched his arm. "How do you know?"

"Our tent flaps are open."

"Oh, I think I left mine that way."

"Well, I didn't leave mine that way, and it's open now." They stood still for a moment, their eyes searching all around, across the campsite and as far into the trees as the moonlight penetrated. David switched on his flashlight and checked both tents. Nothing seemed to have been disturbed. Certainly nothing was missing.

"Do you think some other campers might have come here by mistake?" Sandy asked hopefully.

David shook his head. "I think we're the only ones on this side of the lake for a long way in either direction. But just in case we're not, why don't we walk to the next campsite and see."

"All right," she agreed. "I couldn't sleep now, anyway."

There was a crude pathway along the lakeshore and it wasn't long before Sandy and David reached the next campsite. It was deserted. They were standing in silence, looking out over the water, when Sandy's hand tightened on David's arm.

"Look. Over there!"

A canoe had detached itself from the shadows farther along the north shore — a dark silent shape with two people silhouetted in it, moving slowly out into the lake. One person was in the stern paddling. The bulky figure amidships was unmistakable.

"Max Rogo!"

"Yes, that's him. What in the world are they up to?"

Sandy looked at David searchingly. "They must be the ones who were at our camp. But why? What did they expect to find?"

David hesitated. He was white-faced. "They expected to find *us*, Sandy. They must have. They didn't know we'd be paddling across the lake in the middle of the night. We didn't know it ourselves."

"You mean they wanted to talk to us?"

"At this time of night? Not likely!"

They watched until the canoe merged with the shadows across the lake.

"There are only two of them," said Sandy, suddenly in a small voice. "You don't think they've left the other one around here, do you?"

David shook his head.

"I doubt it. Somebody'll be keeping a close eye on Fred Johnston. He's more important to them than we are."

They turned back towards their camp.

"Sandy," said David, heavily, "I've had enough of this. It's one thing to risk your life for the safety of the world, but I'm darned if I'll take risks for a stupid necklace. We're going out tomorrow, to the police."

* * *

The first light of dawn was extinguishing the

stars when David finally drifted off to sleep. When he woke, the sun was well up in the sky.

Sandy was already up, sitting crosslegged, looking out over the lake.

"Morning, Sandy." He sat down beside her. "Manage to sleep okay?"

"Yes, eventually. But I'm glad I didn't sleep in any longer. It's a beautiful day."

There were several canoes visible on the blue expanse of the lake. Two were moving purposefully, two were drifting lazily, their occupants lying back, and two more drifted while their occupants fished. The sun was climbing in a cloudless sky and a gentle breeze moved across the still surface.

"I wish we didn't have to leave," Sandy said wistfully.

David looked about him. All of a sudden he felt angry; angry with Fred for involving them in his secretive affairs; angry with Max Rogo for scaring them; angry at the whole stupid necklace business. Abruptly, he made up his mind.

"We're not going to let them ruin everything. I don't know what Rogo had in mind last night, but we're safe enough now. There are too many people around for him to try anything in broad daylight. We'll show them they can't scare us. We're going to do today exactly what we would've done if none of this stupid business had happened," he declared defiantly. He thought for a moment and then smiled and added with mock sheepishness, "And then we'll high-tail it out of here and to the police. No point in being too heroic! How's that for a compromise?"

"Good," said Sandy, cheering up. "That sounds pretty sensible. Let's forget about them, at least for now, and have breakfast. Then you can take over. I'm sure you've got some good ideas about what to do with the day."

"Well, let's see. Why don't we combine breakfast and lunch into brunch so we don't have to worry about eating again till late this afternoon. After that, what say I show you how to steer a canoe while we look around for the Penrith's camp. They invited us to drop in, remember?"

* * *

They had no trouble finding the Penriths. For one thing, the Penriths were the only ones camped on the eastern shore, but even if this hadn't been the case, their camp would've been easily recognizable. Not only was their tent much larger than most, but they had also used several plastic tarpaulins to construct an extended outdoor shelter.

Clive met them on the shore while Dorothy waited for them under the shelter where a folding table had been set up. On it there was a cooler, a propane lantern, a radio playing soft music and a camp stove on which a kettle whistled and spat.

"Welcome to Penrith's Paradise," Dorothy said. "You're just in time for tea. Or coffee, or whatever. How was your first night of camping, Sandy?"

"Great," said Sandy, avoiding David's eye. "Did you see that moon? We went for a moonlit cruise. Our camp is very primitive though, compared to this. Imagine living like this in the wilds."

"You can see why we never go any farther," said Clive with a chuckle. "We don't mind transporting all this stuff in a canoe, but those portages are killers. Do you have a radio with you?"

"No."

"Then you haven't heard the news from the lodge this morning?"

"From Little Bear Lodge? No. What news?"

"There's been a murder."

"A murder!" Sandy and David stared at Clive in alarm.

"That's right. It was on the news a few minutes ago. Just the bare details so far. Apparently a body has been found."

"Who? Do they know who the victim is?"

"An ex-convict, they said. Known to the police as the Ferret."

The Ferret! That little man with the neat brown beard and the quiet step — dead! Sandy and David exchanged dismayed glances.

"Are you sure? What — when did it happen? Do they know who did it?"

Clive shook his head. "If the police have any clues, they're not telling. The body was found this morning. They didn't say where. He was shot. That's all the report said. Say, if he was a guest at the lodge, perhaps you met him."

David managed a laugh. "Maybe I did, but I wouldn't know. I don't suppose he registered as the Ferret."

"No, of course not. Silly of me. My guess is it was one of those underworld things — a gangland slaying. I wonder what he was doing in this area. You just aren't safe anywhere these days. Anyway," he added with an air of finality, "it's no concern of ours, and there's certainly no point in worrying about it."

The subject closed, Clive helped Dorothy lay out mugs, sugar and milk and spooned instant coffee into his own cup. "How do you like Canada so far, Sandy?"

David was a poor participant in the ensuing chatter. The Ferret had been murdered! Well, the police were involved now — with a vengeance! Undoubtedly the necklace was at the bottom of this. Again he thought of the canoe silently pulling away from shore the previous night after someone had paid their camp a stealthy visit. Obviously Max Rogo hadn't murdered the Ferret, but that didn't mean he wouldn't hesitate to kill, not with three quarters of a million dollars at stake. If he had the idea that David and Sandy were a threat he might stop at nothing to get rid of them. And if *they* were in danger, how about Fred Johnston? Well, at least Fred knew the Rogo gang was on his tail. But he didn't know there was a third party — one that had murdered once already — involved in the hunt for the necklace.

David waited, concealing his impatience while Clive showed Sandy some of his pebble necklaces and bracelets. He was relieved when they were finally able to take their leave.

They paddled across the lake towards their own campsite, the breeze giving welcome relief from the hot afternoon sun.

"What do we do now?" asked Sandy, troubled.

"I suppose we shouldn't wait around any longer, but just pack up and go." said David reluctantly.

"But what about Fred? Don't you think he should be told about the Ferret?"

"Sure he should, but where is he? He could be anywhere, trying to lead Erik or whoever away from the necklace. I guess we could paddle far enough along till we can see if he's at his camp, but I doubt that he will be."

He wasn't. That was apparent from well out in the lake. Sandy and David turned back towards their own campsite.

"I suppose we'd better give him a little more time to get back," decided David, stirring himself from thought as he paddled the canoe rhythmically. "After all, as long as we're safely out of here by nightfall, there's really no need to hurry. Sure there's been a murder, and that's bad enough. But maybe we're blowing our involvement in all this way out of proportion. Actually, what I'd like to do most of all right now is have a swim. I'm really hot."

Sandy needed no second bidding, and they were soon swimming in the clear water of Loon Lake, lulled by the refreshing coolness into a calmer state of mind.

"Well," said David slowly after they had dressed again, "we should make one last attempt to find Fred. We owe him that much. If we fail, we'll come back here, pack up and head out."

"But where do we look for him?"

"I remember the map he showed me. Let me try and duplicate that first." On the margin of the back cover of a map of Algonquin Park, David made a rough drawing of the lake, then added the X's, the arrow and the squiggly line that had been the only markings on the original.

"This X will be the rock he has already found. It's due south of this bay here, which," he added, looking across the lake, "is just about opposite where we are right now. We'll find the rock and then head due east. The necklace is supposed to be hidden at the point we'll come to when we meet this line, which is presumably a creek. If we haven't seen any sign of Fred by then, we'll come back and leave."

Sandy nodded. "Okay. But we'll have to watch out for Rogo's men. We don't want to lead them to Fred."

"We'll make sure of that!" promised David. "I haven't seen any sign of them all day. Of course, we have to remember Rogo has binoculars. He might be watching us right now."

"If he is, he'll see where we go."

"Yes, as long as we're on the water. But once we get into the trees he'll lose us."

Sandy and David paddled across the lake to the southernmost bay, lifted the canoe ashore and concealed it behind some bushes. Confident that if anyone had been watching they were too far away to catch up, they headed into the forest.

David consulted his compass. "Due south," he said. "Keep an eye open for Fred. He could be anywhere. And so could Rogo and his gang."

The canopy of branches overhead effectively prevented the light from reaching the forest floor.

Growth was sparse and the walking relatively easy, except for the unevenness of the terrain.

The trees were silent, the birds and animals quiet in the warmth of the afternoon. Sandy and David soon began to feel the heat themselves, since the branches that gave them shade also blocked the breeze that cooled the sun on the open lake.

They had been walking for thirty minutes and had seen no sign of life, human or otherwise, when they found the rock, a huge boulder on the side of a hill. They rested beside it a few minutes before turning eastward.

The walking was more difficult now, the hills numerous and precipitous, the undergrowth thicker, with more dead trees lying in their path. They realized it would be very easy for someone to be quite close by without their being aware of it, so they went slowly, trying to avoid stepping on anything that might make a noise, and stopping frequently to listen. It was during one of these brief pauses, just below the crest of a hill, that David caught Sandy's arm, his fingers to his lips.

"Shh. Listen. Someone's coming."

"Where," whispered Sandy. "From which direction?"

David hesitated, then pointed. "That way." He looked around desperately for somewhere to hide.

"Come on." They stood behind the largest tree in their immediate vicinity, waiting, peering round its inadequate trunk.

Whoever was coming was evidently not

trying to conceal the fact. The sound of snapping branches came to them clearly from just beyond the crest of the hill. Then abruptly the sounds ceased and there was silence.

Sandy and David looked at each other anxiously. David shook his head in answer to Sandy's unspoken question. They waited, perplexed. Had they been seen by someone they hadn't seen themselves? It didn't seem likely.

"Whoever it is is still there," whispered David at last. "What's going on?"

It was almost a relief when the sounds came again. Closer. Another pause. Then they came again. Going away. Whoever it was was leaving.

8

The gathering storm

Sandy and David waited a full minute before venturing out from behind their tree. Then, hand in hand they approached the top of the hill and lay down on their stomachs. When they peered over the crest, they found a long leaf strewn slope stretching away from them on the other side. David grinned and pointed.

"There's our intruder. See him? I should've known."

"A bear!" Sandy laughed in relief. "I never thought I'd be this happy to see a wild bear so close by. What should we do?"

"Keep going. He won't bother us."

They went on and after another thirty minutes found what they were looking for — a stream running through the forest. At the point where they came upon it the water cascaded down a stony stairway and then spread out into a cool green pool overhung by ferns and a tumble of mossy logs.

Sandy caught her breath. "What a beautiful spot." They stood on the bank, looking down into the pool. Then they looked at each other and, without another word, removed their shoes and slipped down the bank into the cool water.

"Ahhh . . ." sighed Sandy as she rolled up her

jeans and strode into deeper water. "This is perfect."

They waded around the pool and then sat silently side by side on a log and watched the water swirl about their legs.

"So," said David at last, looking around, "this is where the necklace is supposed to be cached. I wonder what time of year it was when the Ferret hid the thing. I don't think Fred mentioned that."

"Why, would that make a difference?" asked Sandy as she idly probed around a rock with her toe.

"He might not have realized this stream probably becomes a torrent in springtime. If he hid it under that rock it's most likely far downstream by now, never to be found."

"Or maybe some fisherman will hook it. What a catch!"

"Yeah, wouldn't that be something." David pointed to a fissure in the rockface near the top of the bank. "That would be a more likely hiding place." He waded over and felt along its length. He shook his head. "If it ever was there, it's gone now."

"Do you suppose Fred found this spot?"

"Must have by now, unless he was using a tait's compass."

"A tait's compass? What's that?"

"One that indicates any direction but north."

"What? What in the world is the use of a compass like that?"

"None whatever. That's why they say 'he who has a tait's is lost'."

"Ooooh!" Sandy cupped her hands and scooped water over David, but as she did so the log on which she was sitting rolled from under her and plunged her into the water. David reached out to catch her but lost his own balance and tumbled into the water with her. They both scrambled to get up, laughing and splashing each other. Then they froze, the laughter dying on their lips.

A blast of gunfire had echoed through the forest.

For a moment the air was alive with the startled cries and thrashing wings of frightened birds. Then there was silence.

They stood up, dripping, staring at each other.

"That was a gunshot!"

"Yes."

"Hunters?"

David shook his head. "No hunting allowed in the park. Of course it might be poachers . . ." But it wasn't poachers. They both knew that. "Let's get out of here."

Sandy nodded, but they didn't move.

"Where did the shot come from?" David whispered.

"That way, I think." Sandy pointed downstream where the current rippled around a bend. "It was pretty close."

"Yes." David paused, then said reluctantly, "We'd better take a look in case someone's hurt."

Sandy bit her lip, but nodded in agreement. Scarcely daring to breathe, they moved forward until they could peer around the bend ahead of them. David, slightly ahead, suddenly caught his breath.

He pulled back. "There's a man lying there in the water. I think it's Fred," he whispered.

They held hands tightly, not daring to move for a moment. Then Sandy said, "We'd better look. We may be able to help him. Did you see anyone else?"

"No. Let me check again."

David cautiously surveyed the scene again. Just beyond the curve of the creek the trees gave way to an open space and sunlight shone on low bush stretching back up a hill to where the trees began again. There was no one else to be seen. They rounded the corner.

Fred Johnston lay on his back in the water, his arms flung wide. He was dead. There could be no doubt about that. His chest was covered with blood and the water downstream ran red.

"Look," whispered Sandy hoarsely, "he has a gun in his hand. Do you think he shot himself?"

"No, I don't think he did that," replied David nervously. "No handgun would make so loud a noise. More likely a rifle fired from the trees up there." Then he whispered, "Look. Look at his other hand."

"So he found it after all," Sandy murmured.

The Newbury necklace was clutched tight in the death grip of Fred's hand, diamonds and emeralds glittering in the sunlight.

"A lot of good it did him," muttered David. "Come on. Let's get out of here before whoever fired that shot starts shooting at us. We've got to get to the police fast."

They turned to leave, but before they could take a step a voice sneered, "Well, well, well. Hold it right there!"

It was Tony coming out noiselessly from the trees that sloped up the hill, Tony with a walky-talky in one hand and a rifle in the other.

David and Sandy stared at him in dismay.

Tony clipped the radio to his belt with one hand. Then he raised the rifle and casually fired from the hip. The bullet thudded into the stream a short distance from David's feet.

The two remained absolutely still, scarcely breathing as Tony came to the bank of the stream above the spot where they stood. He raised the rifle to his shoulder and pointed it directly at David.

"The necklace," he snapped. "Pick it up and toss it here."

Trembling with fear, David stooped and worked the necklace free from the dead man's clutching fingers. Then he looked up at Tony — and time stood still.

David would remember forever the scene that confronted him. There was Sandy, petrified, beside him. The dead man lay at his feet. The trees stood deathly still, as if listening. There was Tony, nervous, fidgety, waiting impatiently for the necklace to land at his feet, the rifle at his shoulder, his finger poised on the trigger.

And there, not two metres behind Tony — a *skunk*!

The little creature had wandered out of the undergrowth, sniffling and snuffling in the grass, unaware of the human company that stood so still and silent, waiting. David stared at it with sudden desperate hope.

"Tony!" he said quietly, his voice low with suppressed excitement. "There's a skunk behind you — and it looks like it's rabid."

"Save it!" Tony snarled. "Just toss me the necklace." But despite his words, Tony tensed and a tiny glint of panic showed in his eyes.

"It's true. Don't move or you'll scare it."

Tony moved — just a little, so he could look back without lowering the rifle — and saw the skunk.

"Aieee." Total panic gripped Tony. He swung around and stepped back to bring the rifle to bear on the dreaded threat. And as he stepped back, his foot landed on a rotten log — which promptly crumbled under his weight, throwing him off balance.

With a cry, Tony fell full length on the startled skunk, the rifle flying from his grasp.

The spell was broken. "Come on," yelled David. He caught Sandy's hand and started to run. "Come on!"

They fled into the forest.

Behind them, Tony scrambled to his knees, retching and shaking as a sickly odour spread out around him.

*   *   *

Sandy and David ran as fast as they could until they could run no farther. They stopped at last, panting and gasping for breath.

"Thank God for that skunk," breathed David as he leant against a tree.

"I already have. He was the answer to a prayer."

"A prayer? You prayed for a *skunk*?"

"Well, no. I never thought of that. All I said was 'help.' I left the method up to Him. Was the skunk really rabid?"

David grinned. "I don't know. They're nocturnal animals. Usually, if one comes out in the daylight there's *something* wrong with it, but it doesn't necessarily mean it has rabies. Of course this one may have been wakened out of a quiet snooze by the rifle shot. And then again, with answers to prayers, who can tell? I just thought it might be the added touch needed to scare the bejeebers out of him. Remember how he reacted when I mentioned skunks at the store?"

"It worked beautifully."

"Yes, but we're not out of the woods yet. In more ways than one." David held up the necklace, still clutched in his hand. "You can bet Max Rogo will pull out all the stops now," he said as he carefully stowed the necklace in the button-down pocket of his shirt. "If Tony's recovered enough to use his radio, they may already be out looking for us. We have to keep moving."

The afternoon sun was slowly being replaced by grey clouds that were spreading out across the sky. The trees moved and whispered together uneasily. Underfoot, the wind whipped dead leaves into little eddies.

"We could be in for a storm," said David. "Come on."

They went on till at last they saw the gleam of the lake through the trees ahead.

"Okay," said David, "now we go back to the bay and hope the canoe is still there and in one piece."

Sandy and David trudged along the shoreline until they approached the spot where they had hidden the canoe. After carefully reconnoitring the area, they found the canoe untouched, still safely concealed in the bush. They donned their life jackets, lowered the craft into the water and pushed out from shore.

"We'll head straight for the lodge," declared David. "Never mind our camping gear. We can come back for that later. Right now we have to get to the police as fast as we can."

*   *   *

The wind was rising alarmingly. To have headed directly out into the bay — away from land and out of danger of being seen by their pursuers — would have placed them beam on to the high waves which now scudded across the surface of the lake almost parallel to the shore. The risk of being capsized was too great. Instead, David reluctantly steered away from the shore at a shallow angle, hoping against hope that they would not be spotted by Max Rogo or one of his men.

Paddling steadily, Sandy and David soon left the bay behind and moved into the shelter of the peninsula with no sign of pursuit. But it wasn't long before they had cleared that — and then the full force of the wind hit them: a wind that was still rising, still gaining in intensity.

The waves buffeted the canoe and broke in a shower of spray around the bow. White caps rolled by, frothing and hissing.

"It's going to be heavy going," David called to Sandy. "But we've no choice."

He looked up. Grey clouds were moving fast, the lower layers racing with those higher up. Muffled thunder rumbled in the distance. It was a long way to the end of the lake.

David bent to his task. At least he could steer directly towards his destination now. He wished they hadn't started, but it was too late for that. To turn back would be to risk being swamped or even turned over.

In the bow, Sandy was doing her utmost to paddle as David had shown her, aware of the danger they were in. She found that as she pulled back on the paddle she tended to bang her right thumb on the gunwale. She tried leaning farther out. That helped, but it was awkward and more tiring.

She switched to the other side and for some reason her left thumb cleared the gunwale easily. But sooner or later she had to switch back again, and once more her right thumb took a bruising. Then the canoe dipped suddenly as it bit into a particularly deep trough and water broke over the bow, drenching her. She moaned in exasperation.

"Sandy," David called, "you're doing great. Keep it up."

A few minutes later, David called out again. His voice was controlled, encouraging. "Put everything into it, Sandy. We're being followed."

Sandy caught her breath. Surely it was enough to have to battle the waves without worrying about pursuit. She risked a quick look over her shoulder and saw a canoe pulling out from the peninsula. She recognized the bulk of Max Rogo in the bow. He held a rifle.

"Don't worry about them," said David in a calm voice. "They won't get far in this wind."

He was sure of that. Erik might have experience with canoes, but certainly not enough to deal with stormy conditions like these, especially with Max Rogo weighing the bow down. The rifle was another matter, though.

David hunched his back, trying to present as small a target as possible, paddling mechanically, changing sides whenever Sandy did, wondering whether or not Rogo was taking aim at him that very moment. He would be a difficult target thanks to the pitching of both canoes. That was one good thing.

Up in the bow, Sandy's face was wet. Was it spray or sweat? Or tears of frustration? Where was the end of the lake? Somewhere beyond the island. Heavens, they hadn't even reached the island yet! In fact it didn't appear to be any closer than it had been ages ago. Were they making any headway at all against the wind?

Then she realized, the water streaming down her face was coming from more than spray or sweat or tears. It was rain. A sheet of it advancing across the lake, swirling about the island, drenching them, filling the canoe.

Dip, pull, lift . . .

9

Sanctuary

Suddenly, there it was — the sharp crack of a rifle. Almost as soon as he heard it, David knew Rogo had missed. No bullet had come crashing into him or the canoe. This time.

They must be getting desperate, David thought, to be firing a rifle while there were still other campers around. But of course, everybody would be battened down in their tents against the rain. Rogo would consider it worth the risk. And if he tried once, he would try again. David looked back over his shoulder.

There was the other canoe, far behind them. The distance between them seemed to be increasing. The progress that David and Sandy were making was slow progress indeed, but at least they *were* making progress. Erik's canoe seemed to be going nowhere at all. A bullet was Max's only hope of stopping David and Sandy. And evidently he realized that. He took aim again.

A stab of flame and a puff of smoke erupted from the rifle. A moment later, David heard the report — and at precisely the same instant Erik lost control of the canoe. It swung round, lurching and bucking on the water. The waves caught it broadside and tipped it over, throwing its occupants into the churning lake.

David let out a long sigh of relief. "Did you see that, Sandy?" he whooped, "They've upset. We're in the clear."

Sandy looked back at him, her face streaming, and grinned. "Cheers," she said. She hadn't the breath to say any more. Now all they had to do was reach the far shore. Where was it? Somewhere beyond the island. She could see that. And the island *was* a little closer. They were actually making headway against the angry elements.

"The island," called David. "We'll stop there for a breather."

Thank God. She pulled with renewed strength.

Dip, pull, lift . . .

*   *   *

The rocky surface of the island offered little shelter, but at least it was a place to rest. David and Sandy pulled the canoe clear of the water, turned it over to drain and sat down beside it. They looked at each other, their faces streaming, their life jackets and jeans sodden.

"Someday," said David, "we'll laugh about all this."

"Do you suppose we'll be dry by that time? What's it like to be dry, anyway?"

"Rather nice, as I recall." He grinned at her. "Well, so far, so good. I'm glad this island's here."

"Me too," she agreed with feeling. "My arms were ready to drop off. But how long can we stay here? Do you suppose Rogo and Erik will get ashore all right?"

"Oh, yes. They wore life jackets and the waves will carry them right back to the peninsula. They're okay. But plenty mad, I'll bet."

"Then we shouldn't stay here too long. They can go around on the shore to head us off, probably faster than we can paddle against this wind."

David clapped his hand to his forehead. "Oh, how stupid can I be!" he moaned. "Sandy, I didn't stop to think. You're right. They can do that. But even if they don't, we're heading right into a trap."

"What do you mean?"

"Remember those two men camped at the river mouth? Rogo's men? He's sure to have radioed them. They'll be there, waiting to welcome us right now."

Her face fell in dismay. "Of course! I'd forgotten all about them!" She dashed rain impatiently from her face. "So what do we do now, then?"

David was silent for a long time, looking out over the grey, thrashing lake. The heavy rain had swept on, blotting out the shoreline and leaving a light rain in its wake that swirled and gusted at the mercy of the wind. The afternoon light was fast fading. Darkness would come early.

"This storm," he said, at last, "is playing right into Max Rogo's hands. If he can dispose of us, he can blame it on the weather — say they found our canoe empty, floating upside down in the lake or something. But," he added, "they have to catch us first."

"If we wait until the wind dies down," said Sandy, "it should be dark by then and we could paddle across the lake to the forest. Once in the trees we'd have a good chance of eluding them."

"Yes, but we can't wait. We have to move now. If those two at the river mouth don't see us soon, they'll know that's just exactly what we're planning," David replied despondently. "And as soon as they realize we're not headed their way they'll come after us. They'll have the wind and the waves behind them too — and those two men are experienced canoeists." He stared out over the lake for a minute. Then his face lit up. "But then, if they can have the wind behind them, so can we," he added with a sly smile.

"What do you mean?"

"We'll go back the way we came."

"Oh." Sandy digested this revelation in silence. "How far?" she asked at last. "Sooner or later we have to get back to the lodge. Do you mean we go ashore further along the lake and then head on out through the forest?"

"More or less." David stood up and looked back towards the western shore. With the passing of the squall the shoreline was visible again, stark against the evening sky. There was no sign of life.

"It'll be dark by the time those two camped by the river mouth realize we're not coming and then paddle all the way down here, so we'll be able to wait till dark ourselves after all. Then we'll head back down to the far end of the lake.

They certainly won't expect us to go that far. Then in the morning we'll go due north through the bush, out to the main highway."

Sandy brightened visibly. "That sounds great. That way, we should easily be able to keep away from them, even if they do come after us. This highway, is it far?"

He hesitated, then nodded slowly. "A long way. It'll be a tough walk."

"Well, as long as we get back to the lodge, that's the main thing. Meanwhile, I'm starved. Got anything to eat in your pockets?"

"Yup! Some chocolate." They shared hard dark chocolate, sitting miserably in the swirling rain while the water worked its way down their collars, watching the light fade and darkness spread across the surface of the lake. There was no sign of the desperate men who were after them.

Once the gloom had changed to true darkness, they set out, the wind driven rain at their backs. The elements carried them along so effortlessly that Sandy scarcely needed to paddle at all. David even considered stopping at their campsite for dry clothing and food, but the site would have been difficult to find in the cloud blackened night and to do anything but keep the wind directly astern would be to court disaster.

The dark finger of the peninsula loomed up to the right. There was no glimmer of light, no sign of life along its length. They passed it, riding the wind, surging effortlessly through the water. Suddenly Sandy caught a glimmer of light.

"A light, Davie. Fine on the port bow. A fire, I think. It must be a campfire."

A campfire? On a night like this? Who could have started a fire in this soaking rain? Of course. The Penriths, with their sheltering tarpaulins. And they would be 'fine on the port bow.' He grinned. Sandy must think she's on the bridge of her uncle's trawler again.

"Lead on, Sandy," he cried. "Where there's a fire there's a kettle, and where there's a kettle there's a cup of tea."

*   *   *

The Penriths stared in disbelief as the canoe approached their site — a blacker shadow looming out of a black world. Clive left the shelter, hunched against the rain, and ran to the shore.

"Sandy and David! For heaven's sake. What are you doing out on a night like this?"

He helped them pull the canoe clear of the water and turn it upside down. "It's a long story," said David, wiping his wet face with a wet sleeve. "We sure were glad to see your fire, though."

"Well, come on in and enjoy it. Heavens, man, you shouldn't be canoeing on a night like this."

David laughed. "You're telling me! I assure you, we're not out for the fun of it."

The tarpaulins flapped and buffeted in the wind but they provided effective shelter and kept the campsite dry. Dorothy awaited them under the shelter, wide-eyed with questions.

"My goodness," she exclaimed, "you *are* wet.

85

And no wonder. Clive, make some tea, and I'll get some towels. Sit down, both of you. There by the fire. You'll catch your deaths."

Gratefully they removed their life jackets and edged up to the fire.

The kettle sat on a stone close to the flames, murmuring softly. Clive moved it a little closer and a moment or two later it let out a shriek of protest. He poured boiling water over tea bags and instant coffee.

Dorothy came out of the tent with towels and blankets. "I'm sorry we haven't any clothes to fit either of you. You're both so *thin*. But nevertheless, you'll have to get out of those wet things. Sandy, come into the tent and we'll see what we can do. David, here's a towel. Hang your jeans up there over the fire and wrap yourself in this blanket. Then for Annie's sake, tell us why you're out on the lake on a night like this."

A few minutes later they were sitting around the table in the white light of a propane lantern, wrapped in blankets and sipping on steaming mugs. Sandy looked at David questioningly. David hesitated, then nodded.

"I think we should tell them the whole story. But where do we start?"

"You could show them what you have. A jeweller would be interested in that."

"Good idea." David went over to his sodden shirt hanging by the fire and reached into the pocket.

"Clive," he said, as he wrestled with the button, "remember that murder at the lodge you told us about? Have there been any further developments?"

"No, nothing new. Why? You don't mean your being out tonight has something to do with *that*?"

"I think it has." David put his closed fist on the table. "Have you ever seen anything like this before?" He opened his hand and the jewelled necklace sparkled in the bright light.

"Great horned toads!" Clive reached out a trembling hand and picked the Newbury necklace up. "David! Good Lord! Do you know what this is?"

"I think so. Do you?"

"Do I! It's the Newbury necklace. It's been missing for years. Any jeweller would recognize it. Cripes! Why do you think we've been coming back to this place year after year? To find this, that's why! And now you've got it!"

There was an unpleasant note of angry bitterness in his voice, a harsh note which was quickly suppressed. "How in heaven's name did you end up with it?" He added in a more jocular tone.

They told him the whole story while Clive sat in silent awe, staring at the diamonds and emeralds that glittered on the table between them.

". . . and that's how come we're here now," David concluded. "But I don't understand. How did *you* know the necklace was here somewhere?"

"Oh, that. Well, I camped here six years ago to do some fishing and met the Ferret on the river as I was going out. I didn't know him at the time of course, and would have thought no more about it — you meet lots of people going in and out of the park.

"But then I read in the paper about the thefts and the arrest of the Ferret. Of course, his picture was on all the front pages, and sure enough, there was the same fella I'd met on the river.

"My first reaction was to tell the police, but then I thought, I bet that's what the Ferret was doing up around Algonquin Park. He was hiding the necklace. Maybe with a bit of luck I can find it.

"After all, I reasoned, there must be a pretty good reward for a necklace as valuable as this."

"But how could you ever hope to find it in this wilderness with nothing to go on."

Clive shrugged. "I asked myself where I would have hidden it if I'd been in the Ferret's shoes. I came up with a lot of answers — all of them wrong, as it turned out. But I always had hope. With seven hundred and fifty thousand dollars at stake it was worth the effort."

"It's a big park. You must've been very determined."

"Well, it was all just a dream, really, and besides, the camping trips are enjoyable enough in themselves. And now that you have the necklace" — again a barely concealed note of bitterness in Clive's voice belied the shrug of the shoulders and the friendly smile —"well, that's the end of it. But you — what are *you* going to do now, what with these gangsters after you and everything?"

"Avoid them somehow. We hope." David

fetched a map from a waterproof packet in his jacket pocket and spread it out on the table. "Holy smoke!" He muttered. "That's out! I had the idea we might walk north through the forest to the highway. I'd no idea it was *that* far. And dense bush too. Not a chance. No, there's only one thing we can do."

"What's that?"

"Go deeper into the park. They won't be expecting that. Down that way," he pointed. "There's a river flowing out of this lake — actually an extension of the Mattamakos. It leads from the southeast corner of Lake Mong into a series of rivers and lakes that will eventually take us to Brent. There's a railway junction there. More important, it's an access point, so there'll be a ranger station. It's a long way, but I don't see any other alternative."

"Why don't you stay here," suggested Clive.

"You wait here," Dorothy added, warming to the idea, "and as soon as the weather improves, Clive and I could take the necklace out and send the police in to rescue you. Surely that awful Rogo and his men wouldn't bother us?"

"We can't stay here," responded David. "We can't stop in any one place for too long. We have to keep on the move to prevent Rogo from finding us. No, we'd best stick to our plan. Besides, I feel kind of responsible for that necklace now, especially considering the circumstances under which we found it. I wouldn't want to put that responsibility on anyone else — it wouldn't be fair. But if you do want to see if you can get to the lodge to alert the police tomorrow, that sure would help to even things out a little."

"But . . ."

Dorothy stepped in to interrupt Clive's protest. "Of course we will. Just as soon as it's light and the wind dies down. But us old-timers tend to be kind of slow, especially when it comes to paddling canoes, so I think you're right, you should stick to your plan and head deeper into the park. And while you're doing that, we'll do what we can. Clive, why don't you give David one of those little boxes you use for putting pebbles in. That necklace shouldn't be loose like that."

Clive looked at his wife. He opened his mouth to protest again — and then gave in. "Yes, of course," he said forlornly. "Such a valuable object certainly shouldn't be carried loose in your pocket like that. It's sacrilege."

He disappeared into the tent and returned with a sturdy little cardboard box, put the Newbury necklace in it and handed it to David with a sigh and a smile.

David reached over to his shirt and carefully slid the box into the breast pocket. It was a tight fit, but he managed to get the box all the way in and the flap buttoned up.

"Well, you certainly aren't going anywhere in this weather. I'm sure you've given your enemies the slip for now, so you'd better stay the night with us."

"That's very good of you, but we really don't want to put you out or get you involved." protested David.

"Nonsense," said Dorothy. "We've plenty of

space. You two can sleep in the inner room of the tent in the two sleeping bags. We'll move the two cots to the dining area and sleep on them with blankets. Clive and I will see that your clothes are dry and listen for more news from the lodge on the radio before we turn in. Now off you go. You must be tired out, and you really should get an early start tomorrow before any unwelcome visitors do come prowling around."

"Yes, I am pretty tired," David yawned, "and I imagine you must be too, Sandy. We should be on our way by first light — even if the storm hasn't fully blown itself out. Do you have an alarm clock, just in case we don't wake up?"

"Leave that to us," continued Dorothy. "Right now, it's important for you to rest. Don't worry. We'll have you up before the sun is over the horizon, and a hearty breakfast ready to get you off to a good start. My, this is all quite exciting really — just so long as nothing awful happens."

10
Treachery

David struggled out of a deep sleep with a growing awareness that something was wrong. He opened his eyes and stared uncertainly at high sunlit canvas walls. A tent? Of course, the Penrith's tent. He remembered now. They had insisted that he and Sandy get some sleep before starting out at dawn.

At dawn! David flung back the top of the sleeping bag in sudden alarm. It was obviously past dawn. *Well* past.

"Sandy! Wake up." He rolled over to where Sandy lay curled up in her sleeping bag. "Sandy, we've overslept."

Sandy's eyes snapped open. "What? What happened?"

"I don't know. I guess the Penriths overslept too."

Sandy and David's clothes were neatly folded by their sleeping bags. David pulled on his jeans and checked his pockets. Everything was there: the compass, his penknife and wallet. The necklace rattled in the box as he donned his shirt.

"See you outside," he said over his shoulder. David made his way to the dining area and stopped short. He expected to find the Penriths still asleep on their cots. They were not. They were nowhere to be seen and their cots were undisturbed. There was no sign of them, or of the promised breakfast.

With a growing sense of foreboding, David hurried outside. Everything was as it had been the night before, except for one thing. The Penrith's canoe was gone.

Where in the world were they? Where could they have gone at this hour of the day without taking the time to waken David and Sandy as they had promised? He refused to accept the suspicion that was growing, nagging at him. After all, they had taken the finding of the necklace in such good grace. And his canoe was still there. If he was right in his uneasy suspicion would they have left his canoe behind? Besides, he still had the necklace.

Or did he?

He unbuttoned his shirt pocket with trembling fingers and opened the cardboard box. Inside was a necklace of polished pebbles!

"Sandy! The Penriths have gone. And they've taken the necklace!"

"What did . . ." Sandy began as she emerged from the tent, but instead of finishing her sentence, she stopped in the doorway and stared out over the lake. David followed her gaze.

A canoe was headed towards the campsite from the other side of the lake, and even though it was still some way off, its occupants could be easily identified. They were Max Rogo and Erik.

"Sandy! We've got to go. Now. They know we're here."

"How could they?" Sandy muttered, not wanting to believe what she knew to be the truth.

"Find our life jackets, Sandy. They must be here somewhere. And grab some food if you can. I'll go and launch the canoe."

The canoe was lying upside down where they had left it, a few wet, storm-tossed leaves sticking here and there to the hull. David pulled the craft into the water and over the shelving bank till it floated free.

Sandy came running. "I can't find the life jackets. I've got some food though."

"Okay. Forget the jackets. We can't wait any longer."

The river. They must reach the river. Once there they would have a good chance of eluding their pursuers. At the point where it exited it was narrow and tricky. Inexperienced canoeists would have a difficult time of it.

But the river was at the far corner of the lake. They would have to cut right across Rogo's path. In a straight race David knew they could beat their rivals, but paddling at right angles to Rogo's line of advance changed all that. Eric had only to change direction to bear down on them diagonally.

"Paddle, Sandy."

Sandy needed no urging. They both bent to their task, and the canoe skimmed across the water. But no matter how fast they managed to propel the canoe, it was inevitable that Rogo and

Erik would narrow the distance between them. It was going to be close, thanks to the Penriths!

And they had seemed such nice people, David thought bitterly. That necklace must have become an obsession with Clive over the years. David could see it now. The two of them exchanging the worthless necklace for the valuable one, waiting for the storm to subside and the coming of dawn, then stealthily setting out while David and Sandy slept the sleep of exhaustion.

They must also have told Rogo where David and Sandy were. Perhaps they found him out on the lake pretending to be doing some early morning fishing. If not, it would have been easy for them to paddle close to Rogo's camp, greeting anyone there with a cheery good morning and a comment on the previous night's storm.

"Oh yes, quite a nasty night. There were a couple of kids got caught out on the lake. They made it to our camp, though, soaked to the skin. Of course, we took them in and put them to bed. They'd have caught their deaths if we hadn't. Not that I can talk. Stupid me. I left my heart pills in the car at the lodge and now we have to paddle all the way back to get them. We slipped out early this morning. The kids? Oh yes, they're still there. They'll sleep for hours, I expect."

David was jolted out of his bitter reverie by the sound of water sloshing in the canoe. Sandy must be splashing like crazy, he thought. But she's not. She's paddling beautifully. The canoe's getting sluggish. Where's it all coming from? Oh blast!

"Sandy! We're sinking."

The Penriths again, of course. They'd holed the canoe. A small hole covered by one of those wet leaves.

But fibreglass canoes don't sink. They float even when full of water so the occupants can hang on till help arrives. But in this case it wasn't help that was fast approaching.

"We'll have to swim for it," David yelled to Sandy. "Don't lose your shoes. We're going to need them — if we make it," he added under his breath.

Sandy nodded, her blue eyes wide with excitement. "Say when."

"Now." There was no point in waiting any longer. The canoe was going nowhere.

Sandy went first. David took a moment to look back. Rogo and Erik had momentarily stopped paddling, surprised, no doubt, at this unexpected turn of events. David didn't wait any longer. He launched himself into the water from the floundering canoe.

Sandy slowed a little to let him catch up and stayed with him after that, even though she could easily have raced far ahead of him. They swam side by side, catching each other's eyes with encouraging glances but saying nothing, conserving their strength as they knifed through the chill water.

Sooner than expected, the sloping bottom of the lake came up under them. Bad luck. It meant they would have to run further to gain the trees. They would make better targets for a longer time.

They scrambled to their feet, running clumsily, splashing in water that shallowed, deepened and shallowed again, not daring to look back, wondering how close behind them their pursuers were. They had almost reached the shoreline when they heard the first shot. They were on land when the second echoed across the lake and the bullet whined between them. By the time the third shot was fired they were into the trees.

Sandy and David ran, dripping, feet squelching in their sodden shoes, straight into the bush. They ran until they were well away from the lake. Then they stopped for a moment, panting for breath. Water flew in all directions as Sandy shook her head vigorously.

"Now what?"

David hesitated. Now what, indeed! Gone was their hope of paddling rivers and lakes to the ranger station at Brent. He pictured the map spread out before him in his mind's eye. There was Brent beside the line representing the railway, with the road leading out to the highway — wait a minute. Of course! The railway! Why hadn't he thought of *that* before? Suddenly he was grinning.

"South," he said. "We go south. For five or six kilometres, if my memory serves me. Then we ride out in style."

"Davie! What are you talking about?"

"The railway. I forgot all about it. It runs right across this corner of the park: eastward to Brent and eventually Ottawa. But we don't want to go that way. The other way will take us to

North Bay. Or better still, through a little hamlet called Kiosk. There's a ranger station there too."

"Great," said Sandy. "But where do we get tickets? Where do we board this train?"

David laughed. "There are no passenger trains on this line. We hop a freight."

"Hop a freight? Is that as easy as it sounds?" Sandy asked doubtfully.

"It is," he assured her, though he had to admit to himself he had never actually done it. "Even if for some reason we're unable to do it, we'll still have a railway line to follow, and that alone will make things a lot easier."

A quick compass check, and they started out again. They ran where possible, but sometimes it was a matter of stumbling, scrambling, thrashing through thick underbrush and shoulder to shoulder pines that reached out for them with scratching boughs and tripped them up with cunningly hidden roots. They stopped frequently to wipe damp brows and listen for sounds of pursuit. There were none.

Then they came abruptly upon the river and stopped. Sandy looked at David.

"How deep is it?" she asked apprehensively.

In answer, David wrung a stream of water from his sweater. "Does it matter?" he said with a smile.

As it turned out, it was no more than knee deep. They pushed through it and had just made their way into the bush on the far side when suddenly Sandy caught David's sleeve.

"Shhh! Listen."

It was the sound of voices and splashing paddles. Trippers? Someone who could help them? Scarcely daring to hope, they peered through the screen of leaves, and their hearts sank. Rogo and Erik slowly came into sight as their canoe was manoeuvred awkwardly through the water. Rogo spoke.

"This is where they were headed. The river." He swore softly. "We would've been better off if their canoe hadn't sunk. At least we'd know where they are."

"Not much point in them coming here without a boat," grumbled Erik. "They could've gone in any direction."

"Could have," agreed Rogo. "But my guess is they're still headed this way. They'll be hoping some campers will come along so they can ask for help. Pull over to the bank where the trees overhang. We'll wait a while and see what happens."

Exchanging glances of relief, David and Sandy crept away until they were confident that they were out of earshot.

"We've made it!" Sandy whispered. "They'll never find us now. They've no idea where we're going. But before we go any further, I'm going to take off my socks. I can't stand wet socks!"

"I know what you mean," David replied with a grin. "Wet shoes are bad enough without having wet socks as well. It's just a good thing we didn't lose our shoes in the water. We've a long walk ahead of us."

"And a hungry one," said Sandy ruefully. "I forgot to save the food."

"Never mind. It would've been just as water-logged as we are. We'll make it, Sandy."

They were off again, battling once more through the bush. But they went more cheerfully now, confident that they had left danger behind.

Soon they emerged from the dense forest into a wide, open swath. Blackened stumps told their story. Now nature was taking advantage of the unimpeded sunlight and the ash-enriched soil to give birth to new young growth.

They had almost crossed the open space when Sandy sniffed, and grimaced. "Ugh! Skunk," she said.

David nodded. "I'll never smell a skunk again without thinking of Tony. I wonder where he is now."

11

Desperate measures

If David had looked back at that moment across the open space, he would have wondered no longer.

Sick, reeking and drenched to the bone, Tony had found his way back to the lake in the rain and darkness, and eventually to Rogo's campsite. But the fetid smell went with him and Rogo, still angry with him for letting Sandy and David escape, didn't hesitate to order him to leave the rifle and move to Fred's empty tent. When he failed in his attempts to build a fire there after sleeping fitfully through the night, he abandoned Fred's campsite to wander alone and utterly miserable on the lakeshore.

He was wondering desperately how to rid himself of the clinging stench when Rogo came through on the radio to tell him that Sandy and David had been located at the end of the lake. Rogo and Erik were going there by canoe. Tony was to head in the same direction by foot and await further orders.

So it was that Tony reached the edge of the clearing just in time to see David and Sandy disappear into the forest on the far side. He snapped up the aerial of his walky-talky.

"Hear that?" Rogo lowered his radio, grinning in triumph. "Tony's got them in sight. Now it's up to you, Erik." He pulled the canoe in against the bank. "He's that way. South. Take the gun and get after them."

Erik leaped ashore. "How do I find Tony?"

"Follow your nose. You'll find him soon enough. He's not far away. Here's the compass. Go south and you'll soon get wind of him. And remember, those kids not only have the necklace, they also have the power to send us to jail for life. You know what to do."

"Don't worry," said Erik, grimly, "I'll get 'em. It'll be a pleasure."

*   *   *

Unaware of what was happening behind them, Sandy and David continued southward. Thick bush gave way to open hardwood forest where the going was easier and a brook provided them with fresh water. Eventually the hardwood forest gave way to tamarack and pine and spindly black spruce, and the floor beneath their feet turned mossy and spongy. Not long after that the trees gave way to a thick mat of sedges bordering open water.

"We'll have to go around this," said David. "To the west, I think, since that's the way we have to go eventually, anyway." He batted a fly away from his face. "Thank goodness it's September. If it was any earlier in the year we'd be eaten alive by mosquitoes and black-flies."

They circled the bog and pushed south again, the terrain growing hillier, the day warmer.

Well behind them, Erik wiped his brow and cursed beneath his breath. Tony had barely kept his quarry in sight, afraid that the lingering odour might arouse suspicions, so when Erik took over he was well out of effective shooting range. The two kids were moving steadily and Erik had to hurry to close the gap Twice he stopped to take aim, but each time they moved and were screened by trees.

Once he lost them. The ground softened beneath his feet and he concentrated on finding a firmer footing, wondering anxiously if he might stumble into quicksand. Then suddenly he was faced with open water and no sign of his prey.

He located them again after a few frantic minutes, moving in what his compass told him was a westerly direction. They seemed to be travelling purposefully, as if they had a definite destination in mind. He wondered what they expected to find in the middle of the forest.

A little while later, as he laboured over a hill and saw them moving through the valley below, he had his answer.

They all heard it: the distant blare of a diesel horn.

"Hear that!" said David triumphantly. "A train." He hesitated. "Which direction do you think it came from?"

"That way," Sandy said, pointing.

David nodded, relieved. "I thought so too, but I was afraid it might be wishful thinking. That's east, so it's heading the right way. Now, where's that track?"

They found the track a few minutes later winding through the valley, cutting a wide path through the forest. David surveyed the line critically.

"It's not going to be as easy as I thought, hopping the freight," he admitted, "unless it's going really slowly." He pointed westward. "The track goes up an incline there. That should slow it down a bit. The further up the grade we are, the better our chances, so we'll go that way until the train catches up to us."

They heard the baying of the horn again a few minutes later, and soon after, the roar of wheels pounding rails. They turned to watch the train round the curve behind them, three engines pulling a long line of grain cars.

They stepped off the track and watched it come, gauging its slackening speed.

"Should be okay," said David, waving at the startled engineer. "Look at the cars. See, they have a bit of a platform with steps and a handrail at each end. Just the thing for us. First class all the way.

"All you have to do is run along beside the train, grab the rail at the rear end of one of the cars and swing up onto the platform. I'll do the same at the front end of the next car. Okay? Be careful," he added anxiously. "Don't slip, whatever you do."

"I'll be fine."

"This one."

Sandy made it, but David didn't. In his anxiety for her he lost his own footing in the loose stones of the track bed. For a moment he tried to pull himself up, but that just caused him to be dragged along, the stones biting into his leg until he let go. Sandy jumped down too.

"David! Are you all right?"

"Yes." He was angry with himself. "Clumsy fool! Here, let's try again."

This time they both reached the platforms. As the train gathered speed they sat facing each other with the roadbed rushing between them. David rolled up the leg of his jeans, wincing. His leg was cut and bleeding and his knee was beginning to swell.

Sandy looked at it critically. "It's just as well we don't have to run any more," she said.

David nodded. "It's all downhill from here."

* * *

Behind them, Erik heard the approaching train and threw caution to the winds. He reached the track just in time to see David and Sandy up ahead, waiting for the train. He ducked out of sight as the train approached and emerged again in time to see the two make their successful bid to reach the platforms. A moment later, he too had swung up onto one of the grain cars.

Without waiting, he climbed the ladder till he came to the long, swaying catwalk at the top that led the length of the train. Somewhere ahead, two unsuspecting kids sat below, secure in their safety. But how far ahead? He wasn't sure. There was only one way to find out.

Erik slung the rifle over his shoulder,

climbed onto the catwalk, paused to get his balance and started off. They must be a dozen or more cars ahead of him, he decided. After ten he would unsling his rifle and begin checking every platform. They would be sitting ducks.

* * *

"This is the life," said David. "Pure luxury."

"A lot faster than paddling," agreed Sandy. "How far do we go?"

"I'm not sure, but it won't be long at this rate."

The train ran beside a long narrow lake on which they saw several canoes, through more wooded country, over a river, white with rushing water. All the time the sun shone warmly, highlighting dashes of scarlet on the hillsides, sparkling like diamonds on the cobalt lakes.

"Isn't it beautiful," said Sandy. "All we need is a cup of tea."

"I think I could go for a hamburger," laughed David. "No, make that two. Or even three."

Suddenly, brakes squealed and the train started slowing noticeably. "Hello, what's up now?"

David grabbed the ladder and leaned out to look. "I can't see anything, but it must be something on the tracks ahead."

"I'll climb up and take a look from the top." Sandy began to climb the ladder step by step.

A movement to the rear caught the corner of her eye. Curious, she climbed another step — and froze, flat against the ladder, rigid in sudden fear.

For a moment she stared in disbelief. Then

she dropped quickly below the level of the roof. For another moment she just clung there, her heart thumping madly. Then she lowered herself shakily to the platform. Her face was deathly white.

"Sandy! What's the matter. You look as if you've seen a ghost."

"Worse." Her voice was hoarse. "Worse than a ghost. It's Erik. He's up there, coming along the top of the train! And he has a gun!"

"Erik!" David stared at her in dismay. "How in blazes . . ." He must have followed them all the way from the lake. And they had never once suspected. David shook his head in bewilderment. "Did he see you?" he asked.

"No. But he knows we're here somewhere. He was on one knee looking over the end of the roof " — she pointed above —"like up there. Then he looked all round and started to get up again. I ducked down before he saw me."

"How far back?"

"Oh, three, maybe four cars. He'll be here soon. What are we going to do?"

What *could* they do? They both looked at the passing forest.

"We could make it to the trees," said Sandy, without any enthusiasm. "He probably couldn't hit us if he did shoot — not while he's trying to balance up there. And by the time he gets off the train himself . . ."

But David shook his head. "No, Sandy." He indicated his knee. "If I did manage to make it to the trees, I wouldn't be able to move fast enough once I got there. That's out." He didn't bother saying, "You go alone," because he knew she wouldn't go without him. "If you ever prayed, now's the time. We're going to need more than a skunk, though." He looked around in despair. "The train's slowing down too. It'll be that much easier for him to . . ."

The train was slowing! A sudden, desperate idea began to take shape in Sandy's mind. It would be easy for her to get off — but not with the idea of running for the trees. Not this time. They had done enough running.

"David, you pray. Hard. I'm going to get behind him."

"You're what? Hey, Sandy!" Before he could stop her she had swung out on the ladder. "Sandy, what are you talking about? For Pete's sake . . ."

Sandy eluded his attempt to grab her. "I'm going to get behind him. It's our only chance."

Before he could do a thing about it she had dropped to the ground.

Sandy stood as close to the passing grain cars as she dared, hoping that Erik wouldn't see her, counting the cars as they went by, shutting everything else from her mind.

Now. Far enough, she hoped. She boarded the train again, putting one foot precisely on the bottom rung, grabbing the handrail, concentrating on that alone. She couldn't afford to make any mistakes.

As soon as she was safely on the platform, Sandy began climbing the ladder, rung by rung, up to the roof of the train.

She looked at the catwalk, long and narrow,

rocking and swaying, and her nerve deserted her. She could never venture out on that. Never!

Then she saw Erik. He was upright, walking along that same undulating path, balancing, step by step, getting ever closer to where David sat helpless. If *he* could do it, so could she.

With a sob, Sandy forced herself up onto the roof. The rushing wind grabbed and tore at her, knifing through her still damp clothing. The train lurched and bucked like a frisky bronco and the ground rushed away on either side. She crouched, clinging to the side of the raised catwalk. Then in desperation she stood up and started to run — step by hurried step, arms flailing for balance, concentrating on that menacing figure ahead.

Eric had a gun. Even without that, he had far more strength than Sandy did. She had only one weapon. Surprise. If Sandy lost that she was doomed. He wouldn't hear her, of course. The roar of the pounding wheels and the wind would take care of that. The danger would come when he reached the end of the car and knelt down to check the platform below. Sandy remembered clearly. Last time he had looked all around, including behind him, before moving on.

There was a gap coming up, the gap between two of the cars. Maybe she could duck down there until he had checked the platform. But Sandy rejected that idea at once. There just wasn't time. She would have to chance it.

She leaped the gap without daring to think about it. Now Sandy and Erik were at opposite ends of the same car. The next few seconds would be decisive.

At that very moment, David appeared. There he was, suddenly in full view at the top of the ladder, only one car length away from Erik.

"David," Sandy cried soundlessly, "get down! What are you doing?" Then she knew what he was doing. If Erik knew where David was he would have no reason to pause or look back.

Erik had seen David too. He tried to take aim with his rifle but the swaying roof made it impossible. Besides, he had the kids at his mercy now. He jumped onto the next car. The last one.

Sandy saw David, still there, unmoving, staring as if petrified. She saw Erik, confident, bearing down on him. Would she be too late?

She leaped the last, rushing gap. She ran, she stumbled, one foot momentarily off the catwalk, back again, closing the space, losing balance, leaping, hurling herself in one desperate lunge at the back of Erik's legs.

He never saw her. He never knew what hit him. He knew only that something knocked his legs from under him and he was hurled over the side of the train to bounce and smash and lie still.

Sandy saw the rifle fly in the air. She saw Erik disappear over the side. And then she too fell onto the curved surface of the tank, sliding. Desperate fingers clutched at the catwalk, caught, slipped. Then a hand closed on her wrist. Two hands caught and held and pulled her up. She lay flat on the swaying car top and David was there and it was all right.

12
Homeward bound

Fortunately, the train stopped briefly at Kiosk, so David and Sandy were spared the ordeal of making any more precarious jumps. They climbed down, stiff but grateful, only to face what at first seemed like another setback. The ranger station was closed.

Sandy and David were peering through the windows of the station when a short dumpy man suddenly appeared from a smaller building beside the track.

"Where'd you two come from?" he asked suspiciously.

"We came off the train," said David, "and we're looking for the ranger. Do you know where he is?"

"He'll be back in an hour or so. But what were you doing on the train? It's against the law to ride a freight."

"We didn't have much choice. Look, can you tell us where we can find a telephone? We have to call the police right away."

"Why? What's up? What's going on?"

"You've heard about the murder at Little Bear Lodge?"

"Sure. Everybody's talking about it. Things like that don't happen very often in these parts. What's it got to do with you?"

"Quite a bit. There's been another murder near Lake Mong and the two of them are connected. Is there a phone in the village?"

He sized them up for several long moments, looking at them quizzically while he scratched his head and then his chin — and came to a decision.

"Never mind the phone. I'm going to Mattawa. You can come with me. I'll drop you off at the lodge. If it's police you want you'll find plenty of them there."

He was right. When they arrived at the lodge, there were three O.P.P. cruisers in the parking lot and a helicopter was perched on the lawn. A uniformed police officer watched enviously as a couple of lodge guests swam in the pool. Another stood on duty at the main door.

David recognized the latter as being from the Mattawa detachment, a frequent visitor to the lodge's coffee shop.

"Hello, Jack," said David. "Just the man I need to see."

"David! But they told us you'd gone into the park for the weekend. Where'd you come from?"

"From the park," David confirmed. "But we took the long way round coming out. Look, Jack, this might sound a bit dramatic, but there's been another murder. Down near Lake Mong. It's — well, it's connected with the murder here."

"Another murder!" The words galvanized Jack into action. "You wait right here!"

He disappeared into the lodge and a few minutes later Sandy and David were taken hurriedly to the lounge. Several men were seated round a large table. David recognized the lodge manager and a police sergeant from Mattawa. Three other men in the room were unknown to him. When his eye lit on the sixth person present his jaw dropped in amazement.

"But — but —" he turned to the lodge manager. "I thought he was *dead!*"

The sixth man was Austin Webb, alias the Ferret, and very much alive.

Webb was the first to break the silence that followed David's exclamation.

"I don't know who your informant is, young man," he said, "but he's obviously mistaken. I assure you I'm alive and kicking."

But even if the Ferret wasn't dead — and he certainly wasn't — what was he doing here, apparently in friendly consultation with the police?

"The news report said that the Ferret had been murdered," David insisted.

"That's quite correct. He was."

"But you — you mean you're *not* the Ferret?"

"Me, the Ferret?" Webb laughed in astonishment. "Where in the world do you get your information?"

David sat down abruptly beside Sandy and looked helplessly around the table at the ring of startled faces.

"I'll be!" he muttered. "Have I ever been fooled. If you're not the Ferret —"

"I assure you I'm not. Who told you I was?"

"A man who's now lying dead a few kilometres south of Lake Mong — murdered. A man by the name of Fred Johnston. An investigator with an insurance company."

"Fred Johnston?" Webb pondered the name, then shook his head. "What company did he say he was with?"

"Royal — no, Regal Continental. He had a business card."

"Like this?" Webb drew a card from his pocket and handed it to David. It was the same as Fred's, except that this one bore Austin Webb's name instead of Fred Johnston's. David nodded dumbly.

"Then he's a phony," said Webb. "Any of these gentlemen can vouch for the fact that *I'm* with Regal Continental, investigating the six-year-old theft of a necklace by the Ferret. I assure you we have no one by the name of Fred Johnston on our payroll. Can you describe him?"

"Uh — yes." David hesitated, shaken by this turn of events. "Let's see. He was a big man, and, oh, yes, his eyes. Very heavy lids. Made him look half asleep. In fact, people called him *Dozey* Johnston."

"Dozey? Dozey Johnston? Of course!" Austin Webb snapped his fingers. "Embezzlement! We had a run-in with him when he tried to con one of our clients out of a fortune. Do you know him, superintendent?"

One of the men at the table nodded. "Yes. Spent five years in the Kingston Penitentiary. Probably — yes, he was there at the same time as the Ferret."

114

"Perhaps even a cell mate. This is beginning to make sense. And I'll bet we've found our murderer!" He turned to David and Sandy. "You'd better tell us everything. You're the lad from the supply store who advised me against going down to the park before Monday, aren't you." He grinned. "Maybe you should've listened to your own advice. And who is this young lady?"

"Sandy McLeod. Just arrived from Scotland for a visit."

"All right, David and Sandy. Not a very nice welcome to Canada, I'm afraid, Sandy. Sorry about that.

"Well, David, I'm sure you know Art Wiebe, the manager of Little Bear Lodge. The rest of these gentlemen are with the police. Now, what happened?"

David recounted his meeting with Fred Johnston, Fred's reaction to the arrival of Austin Webb, his account of the theft of the Newbury necklace by the Ferret, his claim that Webb was in fact the Ferret and his request for David's help. At this point Austin Webb held up his hand.

"All right. I'll tell you what really happened. His account of the disappearance of the necklace is quite correct. The Ferret was sentenced to ten years. This year he developed terminal cancer and was released on compassionate grounds. Faced with death, he got in touch with me and offered to return the necklace. It obviously wasn't going to do him any good. I was to meet him here and we were to go into the park together to see if it was still where he'd hidden it. Remember, when I came down to your shop to see you I told

115

you I was waiting for a friend? Well, he was the friend. When he didn't show up on Friday I started looking around. I found his body in the bush behind your store Saturday morning. He'd been shot."

"Shot? Of course. That must have been what woke me up."

"Something woke you up? When was this?"

"Just before three o'clock Friday morning. I didn't actually hear anything, at least not consciously, if you know what I mean. I was just suddenly wide awake."

Austin Webb nodded. "It fits. Now this next part is conjecture. Like a lot of people, Dozey Johnston knew about the necklace. Probably he picked up additional details from the Ferret himself, such as the name of the insurance company, and maybe even the general area in which the necklace had been hidden. He watched for the Ferret's release, followed him up here, murdered him and took the map off his body. What happened next?"

David recounted all that he knew, and all the rest of the events, stopping here and there to answer questions, or to let Sandy fill in a forgotten detail, and ending with his arrival back at the lodge.

When he had finished — and had answered all the many questions — there was a moment of silence. Then the superintendent spoke.

"Well, obviously we have to apprehend the Penriths before they get away from the area. You say they left the lake this morning with the necklace? To come back here?"

"I guess so. I don't know where else they'd go. I expect they're well on their way home by now."

"Not necessarily. We've held everyone up most of the day while our investigation's been going on." He turned to the other men. "Pete, see what you can find out about the Penriths. Otto, take the helicopter along the railway east of Kiosk and find Erik. Better take the doctor with you. Sergeant, start planning a trip into the park.

"Now, you two" — he turned to David and Sandy —"we've kept you talking without giving a thought to your welfare. You must be tired and hungry. And David, I notice you're limping. I'll have the doctor tend to your leg before he goes looking for Erik. No" — he waved David's protests aside —"he's here at the lodge and it won't take a minute. Now, how about something to eat?"

David glanced at Sandy and she shook her head.

"Perhaps a cup of tea for Sandy and a coffee for me, and maybe a couple of hamburgers, but that's all. To be honest, we'd just as soon get away from all this and head home."

"Today? I don't think you're in any shape to drive to Woodstock today, David."

"No, not to Woodstock. That's too far. Just to North Bay. We'll leave the car there and take the bus home. I'm not tired so much as drained. After all, we did have a good night's sleep last night — thanks to the Penriths," he added wryly.

"Well, if you think you're up to it, okay. Of course, we'll have to have formal statements from you both eventually, but that can wait." He paused as a policeman opened the door and looked in.

"You were asking about the Penriths, sir? We held them up with everyone else and finally let them go about twenty minutes ago."

The superintendent swore under his breath. "Which way did they go?" he asked

"West. We've notified North Bay and they're setting up a roadblock."

"Good. They won't get far. They don't even know we're onto them."

He turned to David and Sandy again. "From what you tell us, they didn't exactly have your best interests at heart! I'm afraid there won't be a lot we can do about that, since it's all so intangible. But if it's any consolation, we'll certainly get them for grand theft, and we'll do our best to lay as many other charges as possible."

*   *   *

After a hamburger and a hot drink, David and Sandy set out for Thunder Bay. They hadn't gone far, sitting close together in tired but companionable silence, when a car roared towards them at top speed in the opposite direction, heading east.

"Wow!" said David. "Someone's in a hurry. Hey —"

As the car flashed by, David twisted in his seat to look after it. Then he slammed on the brakes, swung onto the shoulder and wrestled the car around in a hasty U-turn.

"What's up? What did you see?"

"That car. Do you know who that was? That was the Penriths!"

"What? Are you sure?"

"Positive. They must've seen the roadblock in time to stop and turn around." David looked down the road. "And it doesn't look as though anyone spotted them. No one's coming after them."

David's car was twelve years old, but there was nothing wrong with the powerful V-8 motor under the hood.

"Hang on, Sandy." He tramped on the accelerator and the car shot ahead with a screech of smoking rubber. "If it was just a matter of theft I wouldn't care. But they tried to kill us — or at least, get us killed. If we can't nail them for that, then at least we can help nab them for stealing the necklace."

The other car was already well ahead, hidden now and then by hills and curves. But as the Buick's speedometer needle climbed, the distance between the two cars decreased. And as Sandy and David drew closer, it became more and more apparent that the Penriths had panicked when they'd seen the roadblock and were beoming increasingly reckless in their driving.

When they came to a steep hill, they took a chance in passing a slow car. A truck loomed over the crest, bearing down on them, and in desperation the Penriths swung back into their own lane. The car they were passing swerved and plunged off the road in a cloud of dust, shuddering to a stop in the ditch. The truck too veered sharply, hitting the shoulder before regaining the road and swinging across it. For a moment it headed straight for David and Sandy. Then the driver regained control and braked to a halt, white-faced, as David shot by.

Shaken, David let up on the accelerator. "That's enough of that," he said. His voice was unsteady and his hands trembled. "They didn't manage to kill us before and I'm not going to let them do it now."

"David! Look." Sandy was pointing ahead excitedly.

Farther down the road a moose had emerged from the scrub pines and was crossing the highway.

The Penriths saw it just in time and slammed on the brakes.

The car yawed madly and careered across the highway, bounced over a shallow ditch and came to rest with a thud against a tree. The hood gaped open and a cloud of steam enveloped the motor.

The startled moose raised its head and plunged across the road and into the trees. At the same moment from the west came the high piercing cry of a siren.

David released a long breath and caught Sandy's hand in a tight grip. "That's it. They're not going anywhere."

They pulled up onto the shoulder and watched as Clive and Dorothy staggered out of their car, shaken but unhurt.

David rolled down the window. "Hi, there," he said genially. "Need a lift?"

The look of total astonishment and then bitter defeat that crossed the Penriths' faces went a long way towards reviving Sandy and David's tired spirits.

*   *   *

The bus wound its way southward, headlights probing the darkness ahead. In the dim interior Sandy and David sat together, emotionally spent, unaware of their surroundings. Sandy had fallen asleep in the circle of David's arm, her head on his shoulder. Her hair tickled his nose and he blew it gently out of the way. Sandy stirred and opened her eyes.

"Skunks!" she muttered. "Skunks and other unsavoury creatures."

"Critters," said David sleepily. "In the best of pioneering traditions, it's critters — and varmints. But who cares. They're all behind us now. Think of what's ahead. Home and peace and quiet."

"Oh, yes. Woodstock." Sandy grinned a tired grin. "Woodstock and The Cow. Now *that's* my kind of — critter." And with that she laid her head back on David's shoulder and slept again.